The

Chris Ord

For the people of Newbiggin-by-the-Sea
A community made by heroes, and strangers who
became family and friends

Copyright © Chris Ord, 2017

The right of Chris Ord to be identified as the author
of this work has been asserted by him in accordance
with the Copyright, Designs and Patents Act 1988.

Further information on the author and his work can
be found at:
http://chrisord.wixsite.com/chrisord
or on Facebook at:
https://www.facebook.com/chrisordauthor/

ISBN: 978-1-9811-2814-3

All rights reserved. No part of this publication may
be reproduced, stored in a retrieval system, or
transmitted, in any form or by any means, electronic,
mechanical, photocopying, recording or otherwise,
without the prior permission of the copyright owner.

'Outside are the storms and strangers.'
(Robert Browning)

Prologue

None of the crew saw the head bobbing in the lapping waves. Nor the shiny, jet black eyes that peered just above the surface of the water catching occasional flashes of light from the silvery moon. The eyes were locked on the ship as it lurched and swayed, its bow cutting through the sea, thrusting waves to its side as it creaked and groaned onward into the cold night. The sails bulged as they clutched at the gusts of the biting arctic wind, each successive blast building with force and menace. Seven sails, three on each of the two tall masts, one jutting from the rear, each tangled in a web of ropes. A long wooden spear reached out from the tip of the brow. Like a marlin, the brig leapt and darted across the surface of the icy depths of the North Sea.

The 'Embla' was heading south, a small crew and modest cargo, hugging the coastline, guided by beacons from the shore. They kept it safe, at arms length, beyond rocks that lurked just below, and others that scarred the harsh beauty of the jagged Northumbrian coast. No-one saw the eyes or the storm, but they were coming. This was the ship's final voyage. By morning she would be fragments, flotsam cast far and wide across an indifferent sea, floating anywhere and nowhere, at the mercy of the waves, all hope and purpose gone. The eyes in the water watched and waited. They saw all that was coming, the end and the beginning. A new journey that began with water, and ended with the crying of the sea.

Chris Ord

1

'How's the catch today, Phil?'

'Not bad Tommy. Yours?'

'Canny. I've had better, but can't complain.'

The fishing boats eased towards the shore, twenty feet apart, gliding across the sea, calm for now, concealing the anger to come. The sun of a dull afternoon in late winter could still be glimpsed as it began its final plunge into the horizon. A chill wind ebbed and flowed in bursts that mirrored the waves. In the distance a wall of black cloud pushed in from the south east, heavy and ominous. Once golden sand was now blackened by flecks of coal, and the dirt and grime of labour. The shore stretched for a mile in a majestic, sweeping crescent around the bay. An assortment of houses traced a line along the southern curve of the bay. The far end was lined with grandeur, the monied who could pay for such a view. Moving north the houses merged with pubs and parlours in the centre of the bay, the small commercial hub of a modest Northumbrian village. Further along was the boatyard where the cobles nestled, and the boathouse that housed the lifeboat. A source of prestige and pride for the village, the lifeboat was a symbol of their bravery, and a reminder of the shadow of death that hung over them always. At the furthest tip of the bay, on an elevated outcrop of land stood the church. It was wrapped in the arms of an ancient graveyard wall, its medieval steeple piercing the sky. The focal point of the community, it was unmissable for miles. God's home on earth, watching over the village, a place of prayer and protection, christening and communion. Where the people were blessed and buried.

Below the church was the spot where Phil would land. Here the beach was peppered with a rabble of upended cobles. Vessels that once graced the sea had now become a village within a village, the homes of the very poorest fisher folk, those left destitute by tragedy and loss. All families lost someone. For every wife there was a widow, for every mother a lost son. The community was strong, they looked after one another, and found comfort and security in all. If someone was lost, the others reached out, took them in, or built makeshift homes. They fed and clothed them and their children. No-one was abandoned or did without, survivors honoured the dead through the thread of kindness that bound them.

'Big' Philip Jefferson lived up to his name. A giant of a man, an ox, with hands like shovels and legs of oak. His round face was tanned and leathery, battered by sun and sea. A thick nest of beard hung from his square jaw, concealing a smile, and muffling the laughter that would most often lie beneath. His warmth and generosity were as large as his frame, and a radiant glow shone from bold blue eyes that had seen too much heartache for a man so young. Loved and respected by all in the village, Big Phil was both fisherman and coxswain, the head of the local lifeboat. A man of relentless courage who trawled the treacherous waters, and led those that protected all from them. Phil had known many who had died, but so many more lived because of him.

As the cobles neared the beach a party of women came to greet Phil and the other crews. Organised, intent, the mothers, wives and daughters of the fishermen waded into the icy waters. Fully clothed, they dragged wheeled carts behind them, with thick ropes cast over their shoulders. As the boats edged forward in the waves the women guided them onto the carts, clutched the sides and began to haul the boats and their precious catch ashore. Big Phil and his two crew mates jumped down into the water and pulled alongside them. The other boats were also being dragged onto the beach, families and community working together.

The weather was turning, but the shift was done, the catch complete for the day. It was time to haul the lines, prepare the catch, then batten down for the night. The community all knew what was coming. They could sense it. They had seen the signs many times before. The wall of cloud crept ever closer as lines of men and women trudged across the heavy sand towards the boat yard, dragging their lives behind them. The women were wrapped in shawls, scarves, and ragged dresses, each face bearing the harsh expressions of worry and hard labour. The shoulders of the women were wide and their arms strong. The muscles on their legs bulged as they dug into the sand, step by step, throbbing and burning with every movement. With a collective heave the boats surged up the final incline and into their resting place in the yard.

A woman approached Phil, their eyes met, and Phil nodded as she forced half a smile. She was small and delicate compared with the others, looking even more fragile set against the mountain that was Phil. It was Mary, his wife of four years, a second cousin who he had known and loved since childhood. Phil and Mary had always known they would be together. Her curled, golden hair had captivated him since they were children, as did the eyes that glistened like the sea on a summers day. When their love was fresh and innocent they would sneak off to the secluded east sands, sitting for hours laughing and talking. As their love grew, Phil would attempt to steal kisses. At first, Mary would resist allowing him to peck her cheek. As their passion and desire for each other grew Phil would reach for Mary's lips. She would play shy, but would always give in. As with all love, theirs had grown and changed. Experience had brought them heartache and wisdom in equal measure. Now they knew every rare kiss was precious, as each could be the last. Mary looked into her husband's eyes and whispered.

'Welcome back.'

Phil raised his eyebrows, avoiding Mary's stare.

'It's good to be home.'

The men and women unloaded the baskets of fish from the boats. It was a decent haul, not exceptional, but more than enough to be happy with. All had returned safe and there would be food on the table and something to sell and trade. Take every day at a time and be thankful when you return. The few days after the storm would be better. They always were. The storms brought terror and danger, but shook everything up, on land and sea. The fish would come looking for food and the men would be waiting. The storm was both blessing and curse and always brought surprises.

The men and women each took an end and carried the baskets up into the narrow streets beyond the boat yard. Children chased metal hoops down the lane, and darted in and out of them, while old men sat on stools chatting and cursing as they smoked their pipes. Some older women and younger girls sat looking on, repairing nets and preparing lines. There

The Storm

was laughter and greetings as the line of baskets weaved their way through the streets. Beneath the joy and light hearted exchanges there was thanks and relief. Another shift had ended, the sea had offered a good harvest and taken no-one in return.

As they reached their houses each fisherman and family dropped their bounty outside, and begin to sort and prepare the fish; chopping, gutting, cleaning, curing. Some would be kept, some would be shared. Most would be sold or traded. The sea took life, but gave them a living. It was the way it had always been, and had to be. There was nothing else. They were fisher folk. This was what they did. It was who they were. There was only them and the sea. The danger gave life more meaning.

Phil and Mary reached the door of their home and lowered the basket. They waved to the two others who shared Phil's boat as they continued down the street.

'See you lads. It's been another canny day.'

'Aye. See you Phil. Are you out for a pint later?'

'Best not John.'

'Ah, come on Phil. We've put a good shift in.'

'I'll see. Maybe.'

'What do you reckon on them clouds? Looks like there's a big one coming? Any chance we'll get called out tonight?'

'We could do. We'll keep an eye out. I've heard talk of a Norwegian brig heading past here. She should have been passing sometime soon. She might get caught up in it. We need to take it easy with the ale lads. I've a bad feeling about this one.'

'We will.'

John winked, raised his free arm in a wave and moved on up the street.

Old Ella, Mary's gran was sitting on a stool by the front door, repairing nets, muttering to herself. Ella claimed she was almost eighty, but no-one was sure. Once you reached a certain age it no longer mattered, you were just thankful. Ella's skin was gnarled and knotted like the bark of a punching tree. Her saggy expression and sunken cheeks made all the worse by a lack of teeth. The dark patterned head scarf she was never seen without hugged lank and wispy hair, while the stool heaved and groaned under the strain of her ample frame. Ella loved her gin, but went to great lengths to deny it. Brave was anyone who took her on, as she possessed a tongue so sharp it could pierce the toughest skin. Underneath the harsh exterior was a loyal and loving heart, devoted to her family and community. She had lived the fullest life of joy and tragedy. There was a mystery to Ella, a puzzle few had ever solved. Both Phil and Mary loved her, looked up to her, as many in the community did. She was an elder, and in the hierarchy of a close knit world that mattered. Phil, Mary, and Ella all lived in a small cottage, sharing the one room as best they could. There was only three now, though once there had been more. Mary took a stool and sat alongside her while Phil perched against the window sill.

'Hi nan, almost done?'

Ella grunted a reply.

'Almost.'

The old woman looked down at the net spread across her lap. Mary spoke.

'Would you like a cup of tea?'

Again the response was little more than a grunt.

'Aye.'

Mary looked across at Phil and they exchanged knowing smiles. As Mary made her way into the house, Phil lit his pipe. Despite years of puffing on it the bitter taste of cheap tobacco still burned his throat. He played with his braces, and rubbed his hands up and down his thick woollen jumper, unaware he was being watched. Phil cast a glance to where a group of children played in the street. They chased, screamed, and laughed, oblivious to all around them. Then he heard something. Music that just caught his ear, the chanting of a rhyme, in the sweet and enchanting tone of a child. He gazed down the street and saw a young girl dressed in a black dress, a ribbon tying back long dark hair. The girl was standing alone, the other children running past her without notice or care. She was looking straight at Phil, her eyes piercing and intense. He didn't recognise her, and he knew most of the children in this part of the village. She was neat, groomed, well dressed. Too much so to be a fisher girl, and the children of the west end would not come here. They didn't even get lost here. This part of the village was known to be out of bounds to all but fisher folk. Phil stared back at the girl. There was no expression on her translucent face and porcelain skin. The pale lips moved as the girl formed the words of the rhyme. Over and over she chanted, the same melody again and again, lilting and dancing across the cold evening breeze. The words drifting in and out as they were caught and swept away.

A sailor went to sea, sea, sea
To see what he could see, see, see
But all that he could see, see, see
Was the bottom of the deep blue sea, sea, sea.

A sailor went to sea, sea, sea

*To see what he could see, see, see
But all that he could see, see, see
Was the bottom of the deep blue sea, sea, sea.*

The girl's voice was soft, but with an underlying menace. Phil was sure the chant was getting louder, as it rolled like waves on the sea. Soon the repetitive music began to weave its tranquil magic, and his mind drifted away with the words. Phil freed his eyes from her penetrating stare and let them wander over the low rooftops towards the black wall of cloud, still creeping towards them, ever menacing, ever ominous. The chill in the air had increased the sharpness of its bite, despite the shelter of the huddled houses. To the north and east the sky was clear, but the dark wall filled the rest, devouring each patch of blue. The storm was in no hurry. Its time would come. It oozed forward like a disease seeping through the body. The full force of the storm wouldn't hit them for hours, but Phil knew there would be tragedy and tears. The storms always stole something from them. Mary returned and handed him a pot of tea, as Phil shook himself from his trance.

'Thanks love.'

Phil noticed something was missing. The music had stopped. He looked down the street and the girl was gone. His eyes swept the lanes, darting in and out of the children as they played on regardless, but the mysterious young child was nowhere. Mary leant her head against him and looked up at the sky. Phil spoke.

'Did you hear that?'

'What?'

'Singing.'

Mary listened and looked up at him, puzzled, with half a smile.

'No. I can't hear any.'

Phil looked up and down the street again. There was hopscotch and skipping, running and fighting, chasing and tag. He heard the high pitched babble of shrill voices, the screeches, the laughter. There was the whining and scratching of iron on stone from the rings the children pushed, but Phil could hear no singing and no rhymes, the sound of play, but no music. The haunting rhyme had disappeared along with the young girl. Mary hugged Phil's arm, gripped it tight and stared back over the rooftops at the black wall.

'Are you worried about those clouds? I've not seen them like that for a long time.'

'Aye. It's going to be a big one. It's moving slowly, but when it comes I think we could be stuck with it for a few days.'

Phil could feel Mary's warmth as she clung to him, hearing the delicate whisper of her voice as she leant close.

'The temperature's dropped again. I thought we might be over the worst, but this winter doesn't want to go without a fight.'

'No. She isn't finished yet.'

Phil and Mary sipped their tea and gazed into the distance, both minds wandering, both trying to cast out what they feared, but didn't yet know. Phil could feel his wife's weight against him, the clutch of her arm around his waist. Phil felt safe when he was with Mary. He looked across at the children again and a pang of sorrow shot through his bulging chest. Wrapping his arm around Mary, Phil pulled her in tight. The future was uncertain, so make the most of now, this and every moment. Phil and Mary knew that more than anyone.

Later that evening Phil was lounged in the armchair by the open fire, his long legs stretched out clutching the warmth. Thick woollen socks enveloped his feet. He wheezed with each breath, forcing out the occasional cough and clearing his throat. Flames licked and leapt up the chimney, while sea coal spat stray stones onto the fireside mat. Phil reached down and flicked the smouldering pieces of stone onto the hearth as they landed, each leaving a singe as a memento. The room was dark, lit only by the fire's glow, and a few candles scattered around the room. There was a strong smell of smoke, tobacco, and the fusty afters of the evening meal. The furniture was a few random chairs, some crates, and a wooden table made by Phil. In one corner Ella sat asleep in an armchair, snoring, an empty glass on a crate by her side. She would spend the rest of the night there. In the corner behind Phil a sheet hung from the ceiling, draped around a double bed.

Mary sat at the table knitting, a candle, fading, soon to die, flickered by her side. She was doing what she loved, what she did best. This would be another fisherman's jumper, the pattern unique to the village, their community. Despite the warmth they offered, the garments were impractical. The wool was thick and heavy. So much so that when wet it was like carrying a stone. Not that it mattered. Few of the fishermen swam. If they were thrown overboard the sea would triumph, and their faces would be ravaged within hours of death, devoured by shellfish beyond all recognition. If the body was washed ashore, or found by another boat they would know where he was from. The jumpers were a badge, a uniform, a symbol of the community you belonged to. Even in death they were as one.

The clicking of Mary's needles sparred with the incessant roar of Ella's snoring. The crackle and bang of the fire fought the howl of the growing wind, whistling through the cracks in the windows, and rattling the rickety tiles. Phil drifted in and out of sleep, his fractured dreams troubled by images of the girl in black. The sweet menace of her chant pounded in his head.

A sailor went to sea, sea, sea
To see what he could see, see, see
But all that he could see, see, see
Was the bottom of the deep blue sea, sea, sea.

'You should go to bed Phil. You could be up anytime.'

'I know. I won't be long turning in.'

'You seem troubled. Is there something wrong?'

Phil shuffled, grasped the arms of the chair, and pulled himself sitting upright. He wiped his eyes and yawned, a huge, bellowing grizzly yawn.

'I don't know. It's nothing, just something I saw today. A girl.'

Mary stopped rattling the needles and looked up, her face basked in gold from the candle's warm glow. There was a long pause. The howl of the wind filled the silence while Ella continued to roar.

'It wasn't her, was it?'

Phil stared across at Mary, frowned and shook his head.

'No. It wasn't her. She was in black, but dressed differently. I'm sure it wasn't her. She looked like she might have been from the west end. Maybe she got lost. She was singing a children's rhyme. I'm surprised you couldn't hear it.'

'That's what you meant earlier. No, I didn't hear anything.'

There was another long silence, as they both stared into the dying embers of the fire.

'It isn't happening again, is it Phil?'

'No. It's not.'

'Are you sure?'

'Yes I'm sure!'

Phil sat upright in the chair and lurched forward. He reached out, took the poker and began to play with the fire. Pushing and prodding at the coals, trying to breathe new life into them. Cracks appeared, the air broke through, and small flames leapt out as the heart of the fire burned bright again. Mary moved and stood behind the chair. She waited for Phil to finish then reached forward, placing her arms on either shoulder. Phil jerked his body brushing away his wife's hands.

'Leave me be Mary.'

'Try and forget it. Put it out of your mind.'

Mary paused and cleared her throat.

'We've got to put this behind us and move on Phil.'

Mary winced, as though a shot of pain had rushed through her. Mary stared down into the flames. After a long pause Phil spoke.

'Go to bed. I'll not be long.'

Mary looked down at her husband, then fighting back tears she turned and moved to the corner of the room. Drawing back the sheet that marked the boundary of the bedroom, Mary sat on the bed and began to undress. She waited a while, listening, then blew out the candle and crawled under the layers of sheets and blankets. Mary whispered her prayers, rolled over and stared at the blackness of the wall.

Phil sat in the chair, gazing at the dying embers. Waiting till all was silent he stood and followed his wife to their makeshift bedroom. Climbing into bed beside Mary, Phil frowned and kissed his wife on the shoulder, before turning on his side. The couple lay for hours, back to back, eyes open, staring into the darkness, sleep avoiding them as their minds churned over the same thoughts. Each wanted to speak, knowing it was better not to leave it this way, as they had done too many times of late. All since that fateful day. As the slow burning fire of emotion faded the couple each fell into a restless sleep, wrapped in the ominous silence of the night.

At the base of the bed the girl stood watching as they slept. A dark shadow with lifeless eyes seeping tears onto porcelain skin. Her black, disheveled clothes were drenched as were her dark locks of long hair. Water dripped from the girl's stiff torso. She showed no expression or emotion, just watched and waited. Her time would come and she had forever.

2

The brig lurched and swayed as each successive wave crashed against it. One after another the waves battered the ship's creaking frame. Ceaseless and unrelenting, the power and ferocity increased with every blow. White swell swept across the deck flooding the hull below. Just as one ended, another began. The howling wind twisted and turned, plunging into the stricken vessel. The sails were wrecked, one of the masts was gone, as the others groaned. Bullets of driving rain completed the assault, peppering the fragile ship as it struggled with the onslaught. Wind, water and rain mixed in a brew of merciless energy. Nature in its darkest glory, displaying majesty and indiscriminate mite.

The crew scrambled to survive, clinging to whatever they could. There was nothing to be done to steer the ship. She was at the mercy of the storm. The men knew it was over. The black wall of cloud pressed down, glaring, mocking, suffocating. Each wave pushed them closer to the shoreline where a line of jagged black rocks waited, grinning like the teeth of a dragon. The captain was Jens Christian, a Norwegian, knowledgable and experienced despite his youthful age of twenty six. He was tall, strong, and imposing, yet little more than a minnow in the midst of the storm. Jens gripped the main mast, both arms hugging it in desperation as the waves swept over him. One of the crew clung alongside. Jens was shouting messages and orders, but was struggling to overpower the cacophony around him. The crew member was just a young lad, seventeen, on his first voyage. The excitement of life at sea now swamped

The Storm

with the fear of dying there. The boy screamed at the captain, desperate to be heard.

'What do we do captain? How do we get out of this?'

'It's too late lad. There's no chance of saving the ship, but I'll be damned if it's taking the crew too.'

If the captain had been able to see beyond his drenched skin, he would have seen the young boy was crying.

'I'm scared captain. I don't want to die out here.'

The captain shuffled round the mast, edging closer to the boy.

'I know lad. I'm going to try to get us out of this. Stick with me and do as I say. Our best chance is to reach the beach.'

They both looked towards the shore. The visibility was poor, but they could just make out the shadow of the coastline. The captain knew these waters well, had made the trip a hundred times or more. He knew more or less where they were. They had just passed the area of this coast lined with golden beaches, but they were approaching beacon point. This marked the start of a treacherous couple of miles with islands of spearlike brutal stone that jutted out from the sea, or lurked just beneath the surface. If the storm threw them back onto that part of the shoreline the ship would be ripped to shreds.

'What about the rocks captain?'

'I'm hoping we aren't that far on yet.'

The wind, waves and rain continued their assault. With the direction and ferocity the captain knew they were more likely to hit the rocks. He continued barking out his frantic words as best he could, all the while choking and spluttering sea water from his mouth.

'If we hit rocks we'll be stranded and need to be rescued. We need to try and raise an alarm. There are fishing villages up and down this coastline, and a lifeboat at Newbiggin. It's not far from here.'

A monstrous wave smashed against the ship and it lurched and tipped over onto its side. Both the captain and the young lad were thrown sideways, still managing to cling on, but with their legs hanging. Jens gripped the mast, but could feel his arms loosening. The wood of the mast was slippy, and his cold, aching muscles were sending bolts of pain through his arm. The young lad was screaming. Jens could see his arms were losing their grip. The captain tried to swing his legs and wrap them around the young boy for support, but couldn't reach him. The boat continued to veer in the wild waves rendering his attempts useless. The boy cried out, fear pulsating through every decibel of his scream.

'I can't hang on captain. I can't…'

It all happened in an instant, a split second, but time seemed to slow. The captain heard the blood curdling screams as his arms buckled and the boy plunged into the icy waters. Jens felt a cold dagger of pain in his chest as the boy hit the water. For a moment, he was gone, lost in the churning swirl, but then he saw the head of the boy pop out of the waves and gasp clutching at the air. As his arms grasped for safety Jens saw the face of a girl emerge from the water beside the boy. She looked calm, a moment of quiet serenity in the midst of chaos. Her skin was the purest white, her long hair, the deepest black. The girl's face was dominated by the largest and darkest of eyes, like pools of water shimmering. She wrapped her arms around the boy as he took his final breath. Then they were both gone, dragged deep into the churning sea.

The pain in Jens' arms jolted him from his shock and despair. The captain knew he needed to wrap his body around the mast or it was over, and he too would be thrown into the depths of the waves. Jens swung his legs up, his boots gripped the side of the mast, but slipped. He tried again, and again. Just as hope was fading the captain succeeded with one final effort. He hung on with every remaining drop of energy while the explosion of noise and energy crashed around. There was a jolt, then a huge crash and groan as the boat smashed against the rocks. The hull was shattered with shreds of wood splintering everywhere, and being dragged away by the water. Another wave hit the boat and thrust it even further up onto the rocks. Jens was still hanging onto the mast, his body hovering over the water. His best chance now was to reach the other side of the shattered remains of his ship and scramble onto the rocks. He could wait there in the hope of rescue.

As Jens began to shuffle along the mast towards the fragments of deck that remained he could hear the screams of other crew members in the water. He managed to reach the deck and pull himself through an opening onto the rocks on the other side. The remains of the boat were still being battered, the cries of the crew still flashing through the air, in and out of earshot. The captain dragged himself further up the rocks and away from the ship, and began to look for his crew. To his right on the edge of the water Jens saw a body. Easing himself to his feet he leant back against the rocks and shuffled towards it. As Jens was about to reach the body something in the water caught his eye, a flash of movement beneath the waves. An arm pierced the surface and grabbed the base of the leg. The captain dived forward towards the body as it began to inch away, dragged into the sea by the delicate white arm.

As the crew member plunged into the water he stirred and reached out to Jens. The man's face was etched in terror, a muffled scream squeezing from his throat. In a final desperate lunge, the captain grasped at the outstretched arm, caught it, and yanked with all his remaining strength. For the briefest moment there was a stalemate, as Jens held firm. It was no good, the arm from the waves looked slender, but it was strong, and the force was too much for the captain. Jens stared deep into the horrified eyes of the man as he slipped from the captain's grasp, and his head disappeared under the water. The captain's eyes were filled with panic, pain, and a sorrow begging for forgiveness. Jens looked into the dark waters, hoping the lad would appear again, but he was gone.

....

On the beach by Lyne Burn a crowd of women and girls huddled together and looked out to sea, their shawls no match for the violent gales and sheets of rain. They watched in helpless desperation as the brig smashed against an outcrop of rocks on the edge of beacon point. Clinging to one another they stared in horror as the ship was broken into pieces by the successive hammering of the waves. Some of the women wept as they saw the dark shadows of the crew clinging to the stricken vessel. A young, big hearted girl, Peggy Brown stood at the front, arm raised above her head, protecting her eyes from the onslaught as she stared at the unfolding tragedy. She turned and shouted at the others.

'We can't just let them die out there.'

One of the elder women screamed back over the wailing wind.

'What can we do Peggy? All the menfolk in the village are stranded up north, and the nearest lifeboat is miles away at Newbiggin.'

Peggy turned and looked back at the brig, sure she could hear the wails and cries of the crew.

'I'm not going to stand here and watch while those lads die. I'll go over the moor and raise the alarm myself if I have to.'

Another of the younger girls in the group replied.

'That'd be madness Peggy and you know it. You'll never get across the burn alone in this darkness. None of us want to see them die either.'

'Then let's bloody do something woman. We're fisher folk, we'd never sit back if it was one of our own, would we? Those lads have wives and bairns out there somewhere too. We owe it to them to try!'

The women and girls edged together even more, many hung their heads in shame. Peggy stared around the group, but each avoided her eyes.

'Well if no-one else is coming I'll go alone.'

Peggy set off through the heavy sand, up the dunes and towards a narrower stretch of the burn. She grabbed a nearby branch for balance, lifted her dress and waded into the icy waters. At its highest point the burn was waist deep and fast flowing, bulging with the winter rain and the fresh deluge. Peggy dug the branch into the bed of the burn with each step. A couple of times she stumbled, but managed to stay upright and reached the other side. A cliff face meant she had to follow the line of the burn towards the shore again and scramble over rocks. She managed to find the path that led up towards the start of the moor.

As Peggy set off across the moor, the biting wind and driving rain were at her back. At times the stronger gusts almost lifted her off her feet. All the while the cries of the crew rung in Peggy's head, each terrifying shriek spurring her on, the thought of every lost man, of every widow, and every orphan drove her forward every step of the four miles in the storm and darkness. The icy wind and rain continued to tear at her drenched clothing. She pressed on, and saw the shadow of the steeple of the church on the point as the edge of the village drew near. Peggy reached the end of the moor and made her way through the dark winding streets to the coxswain's house and hammered on the door. She waited and knocked again. There was the sound of the heavy bolt being drawn, and the door flung open. Big Phil poked his bearded head out rubbing his eyes and yawning, towering over Peggy. The look of panic on Peggy's face soon snapped Phil from the remnants of his slumber. Peggy spluttered frantic words at him.

'Phil, you must come quick. There's a ship run aground on an outcrop over Beacon Point. It's being smashed to bits, but the crew are still alive. You can see and hear them. You'll need to launch the lifeboat to get to them though. We haven't got much time!'

'Come in lass. Quick!'

Peggy followed Phil into the room, as Mary came out from behind the curtain still putting on her clothes. Ella sat up in the chair, her wrinkled face wrought with alarm. The old woman had seen this many times and knew what it meant. Phil scrambled to finish getting dressed, as he gave instructions to the others.

'Mary and Peggy, can you fetch the other lasses and go and get the lifeboat ready. I'll round up the lads. We'll need to launch from East Sands as far across the moor as we can. The wind and waves are against us so we need to get close to the beacon. It'll be easier overland, but we'll need as many folk as we can muster. The lifeboat weighs a ton and will take some hauling.'

Mary gave a nervous smile and nodded.

'OK Phil. We'll see you down there.'

Phil headed towards the door, but as he left Ella grabbed his hand. The big man looked down at the old woman and saw a single tear as it fell from her right eye and trickled down the gnarled fissures of her cheek. He squeezed her bony fingers, nodded then headed off out the door and down the lane, banging on doors, dragging his crew from their hazy, drunken dreams. Mary and Peggy followed alerting the women along with their husbands. All the while the storm raged on, with ferocious gusts hurtling through the narrow streets and piercing darts of rain blasting them as they zig-zagged towards the station.

Soon a trail of men had formed behind Phil as he took the final steps down the embankment that led to the lifeboat station. Phil opened the tall red doors and all the men moved inside. Each knew his role and were quick to get in position and begin to roll the boat out. The lifeboat was a large vessel, a good thirty feet long. It was transported on a trailer with four chunky wooden wheels. The trailer was fine for ferrying the boat up and down the launch strip and across the compacted sand of the bay. However, hauling the boat across the spongy and sandy grass of the moor to the East Sands beach would be a challenge. Even in the best of weather to drag a boat of this size a couple of miles across such terrain was daunting. They would be fighting the treacherous gales and lashing rain of the storm. As the crew eased the boat down the slipway Phil noticed the women approaching with Peggy and Mary. The group were animated, bickering, locked in a heated discussion which stopped as they neared. Mary look concerned as she spoke.

'They don't want the men to go Phil. They think it's too big a risk in this weather.'

A stout woman called Dot, a good few years older than Phil and Mary butted in.

'Look at it Phil. The storm's one of the worst we've seen in a long while. It'd be suicide to launch in this. We're going to have to drag the lifeboat a few miles across the moor in wind and rain, then what? Even if you can get to the crew from what Peggy's said you'll be lucky if any of them will be alive when you get there.'

Phil waited for Dot to have her say, paused a little longer to suppress his emotion, then raised his huge frame and addressed the group.

'Is this what all of you think?'

There were some reluctant nods, and the odd muffled cry. Dot spoke again.

'We've had a bad winter, lost too many good men to the sea already. Martha and Alice have lost husbands and left six kids orphans. We don't want to lose any more Phil. The village has suffered enough.'

Dot paused then spoke again, her voice cracking.

'It's madness.'

Phil looked at each of the crew, most of their heads were lowered. He spoke.

'Don't you get a say in this? This is what we signed up for. We all knew what it meant.'

Phil waited for a response. None of the men looked up or spoke. Phil continued.

'I wouldn't put any lives at risk if I didn't think there was a chance of saving others. This is what we're here for.'

Dot looked round at the others, then down at her feet as she replied.

'It would be different if it was our own men out there, but they're not, are they? You're asking us to risk everything for strangers.'

Her voice tailed off, the words buried in shame. Phil stood up tall, the full mountain of his frame towering along with his booming voice. He was struggling to fight back his anger.

'So that's it. They're not ours so we just let them die. Is that it?'

Dot shook her head.

'No Phil, that's not what we're saying. You know that. It's just we could lose our husbands and fathers for people we've never met. Would they do it for us? Would they risk their lives if it was our menfolk stranded on their shores?'

Phil stared at Dot, their eyes locked as he replied, his voice calmer almost pleading.

'Does it matter? We know the pain of loss. And you're right Dot, we have lost too many this past year. I know that as well as anyone.'

Phil paused.

'But we can't just sit here and let those men die when there's a chance of saving them. It doesn't matter where they're from. They're no different to us. They have wives and children and that's all they'll be thinking of right now. If we've got a chance of saving them then we have to take it!'

Phil's voice faltered as the emotion overwhelmed him. He stopped for a moment, composed himself, and just as he was about to continue a voice from the back of the group was heard. It was the soft voice of a young woman, Alice. She had lost her husband only weeks before. They had been married for just a few months.

'For I was hungry, and you gave Me something to eat; I was thirsty, and you gave Me something to drink; I was a stranger, and you invited Me in; naked, and you clothed Me; I was sick, and you visited Me; I was in prison, and you came to Me. That's what it says in the Bible. We treat strangers as though they were our own.'

Phil looked at Alice and smiled. She stared back and nodded. Tears began to fill both their eyes as Phil looked around around the faces of the women. Most were his age or a bit older. Everyone had lost someone. He could see the mixture of desperation and shame in their eyes. He looked at Mary, knowing she would be feeling as they did, though she would never say it. His wife was loyal, and would always support Phil, even when her heart told her he was wrong and was begging him to stay. The couple had suffered loss and Mary couldn't face more heartache, nor face a life alone, without all that she loved.

The crew of the lifeboat had gathered round behind Phil. They had heard everything and looked on at their wives and daughters. They all waited for Phil as he lowered his voice and spoke.

'I understand how you're all feeling. If there's anyone doesn't want to come with me then I won't hold it against them. I'm going out there, and I need a crew. But if you're not with me then go.'

Phil waited as the women lifted their heads and locked eyes with the men. A smattering of couples shuffled away from the group and made their way up the lane. Five men and five women walked away. None spoke or looked back. Phil surveyed what was left. Fourteen remained. This would be enough to move the lifeboat, but he needed twelve men to crew the boat, and there were only eight, including him. In this storm he couldn't risk launching without a full crew. All oars would need to be manned. He had to find more volunteers and time was running out. Phil addressed the remaining men and women.

'Thank you everyone. I won't forget this.'

He looked across at Mary, her arms wrapped around Alice. For the briefest moment an image flashed into his mind, the image of a girl. There was a long silence as everyone looked on, waiting for Phil's direction. As the image faded Phil spoke.

'Can you make a start pushing the boat across the moor. Try to stay as far away from the beach as you can at first. The ground is firmer. I need to round up a few more men to cover the oars. John, can you lead them out? I'll catch you up as soon as I can.'

Phil scuttled off into the lane, as John turned and rallied the others.

'Come on lads and lasses! You heard the man! We've got a boat to haul and lives to save.'

The men and women filed either side of the trailer, seven men and seven women, mixed together on each side. The four burliest men took the wheels, as the crew turned the trailer round, heaving it along a side road that led to the edge of the moor. The boat and trailer rattled as they made their way over the cobbled stones, still managing to keep up some momentum. Soon they reached the edge of the moor, which was peppered with the dark shadows of tethered horses, left here to graze by the locals. The men and women pushed together without complaint as the wind and rain lashed down on them. Their muscles and lungs burned with the effort, but they pressed on. The wheels hit a mound and struggled to get over it. Pushing with all their strength, energy and determination the crew managed to overcome it and surge on.

Back in the winding alleys of the fisher folk, Phil was banging on doors and pleading with the men to join him. Some were in no fit state to come, while others were over-ruled by the fear of loved ones. Phil had managed to persuade three more to join, all were cousins, all loyal, young lads under twenty, none with wives or children. They had run off to help the others while Phil continued to drag family and friends from their beds. Tempers were frayed, the exchanges often heated and harsh. Phil knew he was running out of options as he approached one of the last doors in the street. It was the home of one of the many in the Armstrong clan. Joe answered the door.

'Bloody hell Phil! What's going on knocking us up at this hour?'

'Sorry Joe, I need your help. I need extra lads for the lifeboat. There's a ship wrecked off the rocks at the beacon and we need to get to the crew. There are survivors, but they won't last long on the rocks in this weather. The others are taking the lifeboat over the moor to launch off the far end of East Sands. What do you say lad?'

Joe rubbed his eyes and scratched his bare chest.

The Storm

'Hell Phil, what a thing to spring on me at this time.'

A young, pretty girl, Maggie appeared at the door at Joe's shoulder. His bride of only six months, a bump in her stomach was noticeable despite the baggy nightgown. The girl held a candle casting a warm, orange glow on her face, the only shred of warmth in the midst of the bitter arctic storm. The flame flickered and faded in the wind, then burst back to life as each gust eased. The girl spoke.

'What's up Phil?'

'I need Joe to help out with a rescue. I wouldn't ask if I wasn't desperate.'

Joe continued to explain.

'There's a boat wrecked over Beacon Point. Phil needs men to crew the lifeboat.'

Maggie frowned.

'What about the regular crew?'

Phil sighed.

'Some of them won't do it 'cos of the weather. The last couple of rescues didn't go too well. I'm sure you know all about it.'

Maggie looked up at the black sky, swamped in thick cloud, the wind howling below and the rain thrusting downward. She touched her stomach and stroked the bump.

'I'd rather you didn't Joe, but I won't stand in your way.'

Phil looked into Maggie's eyes, a silent thank you. Joe put his arm around his wife's shoulder and kissed her forehead.

'Don't worry. I'll be fine love.'

Phil placed his hand on Joe and Maggie's shoulders.

'Don't worry Maggie. I'll bring him back. I promise.'

The look of worry subsided, replaced by a warm smile.

'You'd better Phil, or we'll never forgive you. Now you best get going.'

Joe kissed her, and ran inside to get dressed. Phil stood in the doorway and waited with Maggie. Without thinking, she was still stroking the baby as it slept inside her. Phil looked down at the bump as Maggie caressed it.

'When is it due?'

She looked up at Phil, then down at her stomach.

'The next few weeks, but I don't think it's in any hurry.'

Phil took Maggie's free hand as she continued to caress the unborn child and whispered.

'I promise.'

Joe returned and Maggie watched as he and Phil sped off into the night. As she closed the door a violent gust of wind rushed into the house. The candle in her hand went out. Maggie pushed the door shut, leant her head against it and wept.

3

Jens came to as the waves crashed and tumbled in the pelting rain. He trembled with violent shivers, though it seemed like the body of someone else as the intensity of the cold had suffocated his senses. Within the thunderous symphony of the storm the captain heard cries in the distance, drifting in and out of earshot at the whim of the wind, conjuring a dark, unsettling melody. The blackness of the night burned his eyes. Jens closed them, let the concerto of chaos envelope him. He wheezed and gasped for every breath, each one felt as if he was slow drowning. Slipping in and out of consciousness, Jens felt the cold hand of death take his. The icy tips of its fingers pierced through the numbness and crept across his skin. Death gripped his shoulder and squeezed, the pain puncturing his skin. The captain winced, rolled his head round, and peeled open his eyes.

Through the haze of failing sight Jens saw it, the face of a young girl - a terrible beauty, as captivating as it was horrifying. With skin that glowed with a shimmering translucence, and eyes of the purest black, like jade stones on wet sand. There was no emotion, only the faintest glimmer of life, the chilling vapour of the girl's breath pressed against his cheek, seeping through her pale lips. Their eyes locked together for what seemed like an eternity, as the steely grip of death subsided. Jens' consciousness flowed back and forth, his mind tumbled like the waves. He was trapped in the darkest of dreams, a tomb where the walls were the surrounding storm. The cries in the distance stirred the captain from his stupor. One by one they turned to screams, soaring over the anarchy; sharp, penetrating screams of terror.

Jens wanted to move towards them, but he remained paralysed by the vice of the girl's hypnotic stare. His last few minutes of life were evaporating, then her mouth opened and she thrust a gush of cold breath into his face. It hit the captain like a wall of icy stone and he lost consciousness. The girl's eyes crept up and down his limp body. Lowering her head she surveyed him, her lips hovering just above the surface of his clothes and skin. Reaching down the girl wrapped her arms around Jens, pressing her naked body into his. The girl kissed the captain's forehead and caressed his hair. All the while she stared at his face with the faintest of smiles, oblivious to all around, nestled in the blanket of the storm.

....

The legs of the crew stung with every step, but they pushed on, driving the lifeboat further along the edge of the moor. John was tucked in behind one of the rear wheels, pressing every pound of his solid, muscular frame into the trailer with every stride. He would give out sporadic words of encouragement.

'Come on. Keep up the momentum. Push!'

John's rallying cries would sweep above the heads of the group, whisked away into the night, stolen by the storm. The crew were soaked to the skin, their bodies shivering, streams of icy water flowing down their faces. Their thick, heavy clothes felt like sandbags, but they pushed on without comment or complaint.

The other men had caught up and joined the crew, soon followed by Phil and Joe. The group reached the place where the boat needed to turn and head across the moor to Beacon Point. The going became heavier as they neared the beach, the wet grass concealed soft, sandy soil which sucked in every step, each roll of the wheel. They were exhausted, every muscle burned, and every sinew strained, but they kept heaving and pushing. Duty and determination always conquered pain. The crew reached the edge of the dune, drawing on the last reserves of energy as they hauled the boat over the final mound and onto the beach. Slowing for a moment, the group forced their way through the deep sand that hugged the dunes. The resistance eased as the wheels rolled onto the firmer sand of the tidal stretch, and stopped by the edge of the sea. This was the end of one journey, the beginning of another.

The waves thundered as they rolled and crashed into the beach one after another. The crew climbed into the lifeboat and took up their positions by the oars. The women then flung their weight behind the trailer again, rolling it into the barrage of water. As the boat edged forward the women waded in up to their waists. Clinging to the trailer the women pushed further into the arctic swell, each successive wave threatening to fell them and drag them away. Finally, the lifeboat caught the waves and moved away from the trailer.

Phil gave the order and the crew began to row pulling themselves into the tumbling sea. The brow of the boat was hurled skywards as the waves smashed beneath it. The crew pushed on, developing a strong and steady rhythm as they cut their way through the sea. Back on the beach, the women had dragged the trailer back to shore and looked on as the story of their brave loved ones began to unfold. They all feared the ending as they stood by in helpless terror while the boat struggled through the torrent of water, and edged towards the rocks.

The women began to move along the beach, following the boat as it veered to the left and made its way towards the rocky outcrop and the wreckage of the Embla. Its crew still clung to the rocks, and their wilting hopes of rescue and survival. Phil could see the jagged, black wall approaching. Alongside him was John, both men rowing with all their power. Phil shouted across to him.

'It's not going to be easy getting close enough to rescue them in these waves.'

'I know. The boat is in the worst place it could be. Those rocks are lethal. Remember the last time we tried this sort of rescue.'

John's voice tailed off as the memory returned. He knew Phil would need no reminding.

The lifeboat lurched almost capsizing, as one side took the full onslaught of the waves. A giant surge of water struck them and hurled the lifeboat against the rocks. The crash threw the men to the floor, each scrambling in the pools of water in the base of the hull. The force of the same wave dragged the boat back out into the open sea. The crew clutched at the oars and rowed as hard as possible, trying to edge away before the next wall hit them.

'Phil! Some of the oars are damaged on this side.'

Phil looked across and could see the oars flapping in the hands of two of the crew. He stared down at the base of the hull and saw water flooding in through a rip in the side. Splinters of wood floated in the growing pool at the crew's feet. Another strong wave smashed into the lifeboat and thrust them back onto the rocks again. There was another crunch as the men were strewn across the boat once more. The crew struggled to dis-entangle themselves from crumpled heaps, with several crawling on their hands and knees through the rising water towards their oars. There was shouting and cursing, all mixed with the cacophonous din of the wind and waves. John grabbed Phil by the shoulder and pushed his face close.

'It's no use Phil. If we stay here we'll be wrecked too. I've never known it this bad. There's no way we'll get onto those rocks in one piece, and even if we do, how're we going to get off?'

Phil looked down at the water in the hull. It was now approaching their knees. The rescue was always a huge risk, but the damage to the boat had crippled them. It wasn't just the lives of the strangers at stake now, but Phil's family and friends, loved ones in the community. The image of Maggie flashed into Phil's head. She was standing next to him, stroking her stomach. He remembered the promise, tasted the words as they left his lips. He scanned the line of men all sat at the oars, arms pumping in desperation, determined to overcome the power of the waves and move away from the rocks. Phil saw Joe at the back of the boat, face wrought with pain and determination. Joe was just a boy, a father to be, someone who deserved a future, and right now that future depended on Phil.

Phil saw a girl standing at the back of the boat. As she had always been. Dressed in black clothes, long dark hair soaking wet, her tiny curls and ringlets dripping. Even in the depths of the night Phil could make out the girl's eyes. The blackest crystals that seemed to pierce the enveloping darkness, reaching out and clutching at his own. The girl's skin glowed a bluey white. She did nothing, just stared at Phil. This was as she always came to him. At first in his dreams, then more often in the waking world. The girl grew bolder, more brazen with every haunting, and now appeared even when there were others around. It had been a while though. Phil thought it was over, but the girl had returned, and he knew why. Phil wiped water from his drenched face and she was gone.

Phil hauled himself to the front of the lifeboat and looked across at the rocks, where he could make out the wreckage of the Embla. One of the masts had collapsed, the main one was still perched aloft, swaying. Pieces of timber were scattered everywhere. The lifeboat tumbled in the rise and fall of the waves, but Phil could just see the shadows of bodies. There was more though, something alongside them, what looked like naked bodies. Glowing an eery dreamlike light, they looked like human lanterns with long black hair stretched down their backs. None of the crew of the Embla moved as the luminous figures leant over them. Phil shook his head and wiped his eyes just as another massive wave hit the lifeboat. They lunged towards the wall of stone again, just missing another crashing blow. Phil knew he needed to act soon. If the lifeboat hit the rocks once more it would be over.

....

On the beach the women looked on, frantic as they watched the lifeboat smashing against the black jaws of Beacon Point. There were gasps and screams, while many wept. They could see the wreck of the Embla, but only Mary and Peggy had noticed the strange lights. Faint and distant in the blackness of the night sky they looked like small fireflies peppering the rocks. Peggy huddled close to Mary wrapping her drenched shawl around her shoulders. She screamed above the roar of the wind and waves.

'What are those lights on the rocks? Do you see them?'

'Yes. I've no idea. It might be something from the ship, something in its cargo.'

Mary was neither convincing nor convinced. They both looked on, mesmerised by the faint, eery glow, but at the same time horrified by the sight of the lifeboat being tossed and turned in the waves like a toy.

....

Phil continued to scour the rocks, puzzled by the strange shapes and lights, and troubled by the decision to continue or abandon the rescue. There was a new noise, a chilling sound coming from the rocks. It was faint at first, ebbing on the waves of the wind and battling through the chaos of the storm. Phil heard it again, clearer this time, unmistakable. It was wailing and screams, but not screams for help, these were different. These were terrifying blood curdling screams of shock and terror. Phil turned to John who was now by his side.

'Do you hear that John? That sound. Screams. There are men still alive out there.'

'I don't hear anything Phil. You're probably imagining it.'

Phil grabbed his friend's shoulder.

'Listen man. You can hear it. Look. See those shadows and lights? It's coming from them.'

John listened, stared, and shook his head.

'I don't hear or see anything. There's only this bloody storm. Chances are they're all dead and if we don't get out of here soon, it'll be us too. Come on Phil, don't fight this. It's over.'

John looked up at Phil pleading through dripping eyes. The two men had been friends for many years. They had grown up together almost as brothers. John knew Phil's courage better than any man, but also shared his heartache. John knew what was driving his friend to this. He knew why this was so important. John knew why Phil refused to give up. Phil tried to respond, but his voice was cracking with the desperation and emotion.

'But I can hear them John, I can see them. There are men still alive who need us. I can't let them die.'

John took his arm and stared at his friend.

'It's over. Don't make these young lads and their families suffer like you have.'

Phil bowed his head, shaking and nodding, mumbling to himself. John looked on and waited. Suddenly Phil jumped up, looking alert and determined, barking out orders to the crew as he moved back to man his oar followed by John.

'Let's get back to the beach lads. It's finished. We'll never reach the rocks in this. We've done all we can.'

....

The women waited, hanging on in desperation, slow dying with every breath. Hoping. Praying. It was Mary who noticed it first, the change in direction as the lifeboat began to edge away from the rocks. It was moving back along the line of the coast and towards the beach. Mary shouted over the din of the storm.

'They're leaving. Look!'

Relief swept through the group as they huddled even closer, holding each other tight. The women knew the lifeboat was still in danger, but return was much safer than rescue. The tyranny of the Beacon was legendary. Local fishermen revered and feared the area, as much as they did nature itself. On nights like this, all were reminded that humanity had not conquered nature, and never would. The tension lifted from the group with every stroke of the oars. Layer after layer the relief peeled from the women's bodies. Breath after breath they felt alive again as the lifeboat moved towards the safety of the beach. The women ran back to the trailer and prepared to launch it into the water once more that night. This time it was a welcome not farewell, relief had now replaced fear. Loved ones would soon be back, safe and sound as Phil had promised.

....

The screams stopped as they had begun. All that was left was the terror of the storm, the waves, the wind, and the rain. The shattered splinters of the 'Embla' continued to hammer against the rocks as the waves played with its shattered remains. The once mighty vessel was now just flotsam scattered on the rocks and surrounding sea. Amongst the fragments the strange translucent lights wrapped themselves around the lifeless shadows. The lights lifted their bounty and slid towards the sea dragging the crew in their arms. Slow, delicate, gentle, one after another light and shadows slipped into the pounding waves and plunged deep into the dark depths. Only nature's brutal symphony remained, its raw power savage and remorseless. Unforgiving.

....

Scraps of morning light seeped through the black clouds as the storm raged on. It showed no sign of easing. The wreckage of the Embla rocked and swayed, still struck by wind and wave. The crew had gone and only the shattered hull remained. In the village the fishermen and women slept, exhausted from the night before. All but Phil. He sat up all night, racked with guilt and remorse, the image of the girl in his mind, saying prayers over and over. Prayers for the souls of the lost men he couldn't save.

The rain lashed down upon the beach of East Sands. Fragments of the Embla had washed upon the shore, tangled in bright green kelp, while flotsam still churned in the pounding waves. Lying on the cold damp sands was a naked body draped in long black hair. It was the body of a young girl with smooth, white skin tinged with pale blue. Curled in a ball, the girl lay still, like a foetus in the womb. Her small chest moved with the gentle rhythm of breathing. The arctic wind brushed over her naked body, as the icy rain beat down, but she remained still, oblivious to the terror of the storm. It was her protection, not harm. It had come for her, and she waited to be found, seeking to be born. Again. Somewhere in the distance, way off in the midst of the swirling waves was a cry. It was the cry of the sea. Her time was about to come.

DAY ONE

Chris Ord

4

Phil stood by the doorway puffing on his pipe. The wall of cloud still hung above the village and beyond, smothering the light of the early morning sun. The wind howled and the rain pounded down, wave after wave of razor sharp bullets stinging the skin. Phil felt nothing though. Numbed by images of the night before, his mind was locked on the dark shadows and shimmering lights on the rocks, of the terror and bravery of his young crew. He kept telling himself what might have been, his blessing and curse, the path he had chosen. He looked to save, to preserve life and cheat death, but in doing so he walked the finest of lines. Sometimes he lost.

He made his way through the streets and towards the edge of the moor. The top end of the village was silent. This was unusual, but there would be no catch today, not until the storm faded. Reaching the long grass of the moor, damp and heavy, Phil trudged on towards the beach of East Sands. Horses stood, heads bowed, cold, wet, miserable. Tethered to iron spikes on threadbare ropes, their home was no more than a small circular piece of grazing land. Poor creatures. Trapped and exposed to all the elements could hurl at them, at the mercy of man and nature. At the edge of the dunes he cut through a narrow gap in the long, sharp spears of grass, his massive feet pounding the heavy sand. An icy blast of wind struck his face as he left the shelter of the dunes and moved onto the narrow stretch of beach.

Phil slowed as he reached the waterline, head bowed combing the waves and dark wet sand. The tide was high, the waves at their most ferocious, but the eyes kept searching. There was something, further down the beach, a black object, a jacket. Leaning down, Phil searched through the pockets, and found papers in one. They were soaked and stuck together, the ink blurred and washed out. Placing them in his overcoat, Phil laid the jacket out on the sand and moved on through the rocks and pebbles, the seaweed and fragments of wood. The sands were littered with debris, much of it remnants of the tragedy. There were no crew, no bodies to gather, no corpses to take back, to be laid out, to pay respects to and say prayers for. There were none to be buried. He pressed on, knowing this was only the beginning even though the beach was coming to an end.

Something caught his eye. At the far end of the sands near the edge of the first stretch of rocks. Again it was black, but this was different. Phil stepped up the pace of his large, bounding steps, his massive frame leaving deep imprints in the sand. As he neared, Phil saw her. Long black hair hung across a naked back, nestled on the beach. Flecks of golden sand clung to the black strands as they lay draped across her pale body. The girl's arms were wrapped around her thighs and lower legs, as she lay curled in a ball. Phil slowed as he approached the still body. The bluey whiteness of her skin gave every impression of death. He watched and waited, then lowered his stiff legs and reached out his hand to touch her arm. The skin was ice cold, but still soft and supple. Running his fingers towards her hair, he could see the delicate breathing, her back and shoulders creeping in and out. Placing his hand on her shoulder, he began to close his fingers into a gentle grip around it, careful not to hurt or alarm her, hoping it might stir the girl. Suddenly, she moved, sitting with a jolt and scrambling across the sands away from him. The girl's dark eyes gazed back at him in fear, her pink lips trembling. Even the mask of terror could not disguise the purity of the girl's face and intensity of her beauty.

Phil smiled and eased his hand towards her.

'Don't worry. I won't hurt you.'

As his hand touched her leg she flinched and shuffled away, her eyes still locked on his.

'It's OK. I'm here to help. You must be freezing. Here take this.'

He eased himself to his feet and removed his long heavy overcoat, kneeling forward and laying it across the girl. She didn't move, but he felt her quivering as he wrapped the coat around her. All the while those dark, penetrating eyes never left his, locked in terror, but tinged with a frailty and innocence.

'Do you speak English?'

There was no response, not even a sign that she understood. Phil spoke again, this time trying to act out the words with flimsy gestures.

'You need to come with me. I'll take you home and get you warmed, dressed and fed. You can't stay out here. You'll freeze to death. Can I?'

Phil leant forward and lowered his arms under the girl, lifting her into the cradle of his chest, wrapped in the blanket of the thick overcoat. Her head rested on his shoulder, her face so close he could feel the cold stroke of every breath as it brushed against his cheek. The shivering eased as Phil carried her back along the sands, trying to shelter her from the ravages of the storm. The girl was as light as air, slender, little more than a rag doll in his arms. He stared at the ground in front, keen to avoid hazards and her stare. Those dark eyes were beguiling and disturbing. There was something hypnotic, but unsettling simmering within them.

They moved through the dunes, back across the moor towards the narrow lanes of home. It was still early, but more people had stirred and were up and about their business. Phil exchanged good mornings with each person as they passed, seeing the looks of shock and bemusement sweep across their faces when they saw the bundle in his arms. He reached his house and paused before turning the handle. The door creaked open, and lowering his head Phil stepped inside. Ella was in her chair, while Mary placed fresh coals on the roaring fire. Both looked up, aghast when they saw Phil towering in the doorway, the small, delicate creature wrapped in his arms. The girl's tiny head rested on his shoulder, as the deep, dark eyes peered out over Phil's jacket. At first Phil said nothing, gesturing to Mary with his eyes, hoping the alarm on her face would ease and she would take control. Mary was the master of these situations. She knew what to do, and acted without any fuss. This had stunned even her. After a long pause Phil filled the awkward silence.

'I found her on the beach. She must be from the ship. She's got no clothes and she's freezing.'

'Quick! Bring her here by the fire.'

Mary sprung into action as Phil placed the girl in the chair, filling the kettle and setting the water to boil on the fire. They all stared at the girl, waiting for the water to boil, then watched in silence as Mary prepared the tea. Phil shuffled away, looking at Ella who remained in her chair in the corner. The look of shock on Ella's face had eased, replaced with a suspicious scowl. There was an edge to Ella's expression Phil had not seen before, a sharpness in her look that suggested she was nervous and wary. Ella took her time with people, was always cautious at first, especially so with strangers. Family was everything. The home their sanctuary.

Mary passed the tea to the girl who just stared at the cup.

'It's tea. Take it. It'll do you good. You must've had a terrible night.'

The girl looked back at Mary puzzled, showing no sign of understanding or taking the tea. Mary laid the cup on the hearth beside the girl's chair and went behind the curtain of the bedroom area. She returned with some clothes, underwear, socks, a crimson dress, and black cardigan. Mary laid them on the arm of the chair beside the girl.

'Here, put these on. You need to get warmed through.'

The girl's head moved and eyes followed, but there was no response. Mary spoke again, her words slower, more pronounced, all the while her face reassuring the girl.

'Put these on. Please.'

The final word hung in the air, echoed. It was a heartfelt plea, steeped in Mary's warmth and caring. Mary looked down at her, and waited. There was nothing, no movement or acknowledgement, only a vacant stare still tinged with fear. Mary wasn't prepared to wait any longer and reached down and removed the jacket. Casting a cutting glance back at Phil, Mary helped the girl to her feet, as her naked body was now on full view. Phil felt the force of Mary's stare and turned away as she began to dress the girl. Mary was delicate and gentle, as if she were dressing a much younger child. Phil looked at the floor and shuffled his feet, in clumsy awkward motions. Ella looked on, switching her stare between Phil and Mary, cornering him with her judgmental scowl. There was a knock at the door, and Phil opened it to find John, face dripping with water from the rain, fresh droplets hanging from his nose and chin. The neighbour's hands were pressed deep into the pockets of his heavy overcoat, a flat cap and lowered head obscuring his eyes and the top half of his face.

'Morning Phil.'

'Morning John. What's up?'

'There's word going round you've found someone. Is it a survivor?'

John eyes ducked and darted from side to side, trying to find their way around the large mound of flesh that filled the doorway, hoping to glimpse what lay inside. Phil edged forward, pushing outside, forcing his friend to move back into the yard. The big man pulled the door shut behind him.

'I might've known news would travel fast. Nothing gets missed around here, does it? Yes. I found someone on the beach. A young girl. So far she's the only survivor. There was no-one else, not even any bodies.'

His voice tailed off to a whisper, as John replied fizzing with excitement.

'A girl! Who? Has she said where she's from?'

'She hasn't said a thing so far. She's probably in shock, and I doubt she speaks much English anyway. The Embla was Norwegian so there's not much chance of anyone round here being able to understand her.'

John shook his head.

'Nah. Them buggers at the West End can't even understand us half the time.'

They both grinned, the thin glimmer of humour soon subsiding as John spoke again.

'It's a bloody miracle she got through the night in this weather.'

Phil nodded.

'It is, and she was naked when I found her too.'

'What? Not a stitch on? In this weather? No-one could survive the sea and then a night on the beach naked Phil.'

Both men's eyes caught one another, each understood what the other was thinking. John looked awkward and uncomfortable as he continued.

'So what are you going to do with her?'

'I'll take her to Morpeth, hand her over to the magistrates. There'll be someone who can find out what they need from the shipping companies. There should be records of the crew and any passengers.'

Phil looked up at the skies, as the thick black clouds continued to smother the village. John followed the line of Phil's gaze, pulled up the collar of his jacket and dragged his hat down on his head.

'You won't get anywhere in a hurry until this storm lifts.'

'I know. She'll have to stay with us till the weather turns. She should be fine for a day or so. We'll get everyone to rally round.'

There was a pause, as the silence between the two friends was filled with the sounds of the storm. It was picking up power again, cascading around them. John looked at Phil, his eyes forming words his lips wouldn't. Phil knew what he wanted to ask.

'Look John. I'd love to invite you in, but Mary's getting the girl dressed. She'll then need some food and rest. You understand, eh mate?'

Phil smiled at his friend, his oldest and dearest, as he placed his hand on his shoulder. John nodded.

'I've got you Phil. I just wanted to see if there's anything I could do to help. Just give me a shout if you need anything. Are you heading down for a drink later? We've earned a few after last night eh?'

'Aye. I'll try and get down for a couple. Once things settle down here. Oh, and about last night John. Thanks mate. You know I appreciate it. We did our best.'

Phil reached out his hand, as John looked up and smiled, the friends gripping each other in a long, lingering shake that filled the vacuum of words.

Both men said their farewells, then John lumbered off through the wind and rain to the warmth and comfort of his own cottage. Phil moved back inside where the girl sat in the armchair gazing into the heart of the fire. She was wearing Mary's clothes, a dress familiar to Phil, the one she wore when they first married. Phil paused as his mind wandered for a moment, lost in a daydream, a memory of a forgotten past. A faint smile crept across his lips, then the darkness swept in again, thoughts of more recent times. Phil felt the pain of loss surge through him. Mary was at the table preparing some food. She looked up at Phil, saw his anguished expression.

'Phil. Come here a second, will you?'

Phil was startled, and looked at Mary to see her beckoning him over with a flick of her head. They both huddled in the far corner of the room. Mary looked back at the girl and Ella, then spoke in the softest of whispers.

'What are we going to do with her Phil? The poor girl's in shock. She probably needs to see a doctor. Was she like that when you found her?'

'Yes. She was lying on the sand, curled in a ball. She had nothing on. She was just as I brought her. I'll have to take her to Morpeth, but I won't get far in this. The trip's too dangerous in this weather. She'll have to stay with us until the storm clears. It might only be a day or two.'

Mary looked concerned, as she leant back casting another glance over to the girl. She sat in the chair, motionless, still mesmerised by the fire, silent and staring. Meanwhile, Ella looked on, watching, the scowl still etched on her face. There was a long silence as Mary was locked deep in thought. Phil looked on, waiting for his wife to answer. Mary looked at her husband and frowned.

'I'm not happy about this Phil, but I suppose there's nothing else we can do. As soon as the weather turns you'll have to take her.'

Mary paused and lowered her voice.

'There's something about her. I can't put my finger on it, but there's something not right.'

Phil scowled.

'Don't Mary.'

'Do you blame me? You must have thought it too. I mean look at her.'

Mary shook her head.

'She can stay for now. We've not got much choice. We can't turn her out into the streets.'

The couple's eyes locked, exchanging a knowing sadness, a shared tragedy they no longer mentioned. Phil spoke.

'I'll sort everything as soon as I can.'

Mary forced a smile, as Phil lifted his hand and brushed the hair from his wife's face, his hand lingering against her soft skin. He spoke, his voice barely above a whisper.

'I know it hasn't been easy for you Mary, for any of us.'

Mary stared at the floor, fighting back the tears. Phil looked down at her.

'If I could go back and make things right I would you know that, don't you?'

Mary nodded.

'I know.'

There was a long silence as the couple pondered what might have been. Mary took out a handkerchief and wiped her eyes, then stared across at the girl, and whispered again.

'You can't help wondering though, can you?'

'What?'

'How anyone could survive that freezing water, then a whole night on the beach, naked in this weather. There's something strange about it.'

Mary's gaze remained locked on the girl, while Phil's thoughts drifted back to the beach, and the moment he discovered the girl. She lay on the sand like an unborn child, still as stone in the deathly cold. The wind and rain beat down. All the while Phil watched as the weather ravaged her naked body, her delicate frame wrapped in the dark blanket of black hair. The only movement was the steady pulse of her gentle breathing. There were no shivers. The girl lay still. The images of the morning dissolved and Phil spoke.

'I've no idea how she could have survived that. No idea at all.'

5

The bar was dark and smoky, reeking of tobacco and ale. The fishermen huddled round rows of rickety tables, sat on wooden benches exchanging bawdy laughter and animated discussion. A group were singing; loud, raucous, and only just in tune. A traditional sea shanty, the self appointed choirmaster was up on his feet urging more of the bar to join in. Most shrugged him off, while some would wail for a couple of lines. This was a sea of masculinity, where men came to escape, talk about the forbidden, matters reserved for the ears of their own.

Phil and John sat in the corner furthest away from the door. They were joined by two others, both crew of the lifeboat, younger men, rookies. Phil sat upright smoking his pipe and knocking back the occasional swig of bitter ale. John was opposite, already worse for wear. Phil could drink all day without the slightest impact, but with John, one or two pints and his speech would slur, and voice lift in volume and pitch. He remained like that for the rest of the evening, never worse or to the point of collapse, always teetering on the edge of chaos and control. Joe Arkle, a young lad new to the lifeboat crew was dominating the discussions along with John, while Phil and Jack Smith listened. Joe's youthful looks were flush with the ale and passion of his talk. His long curled mop of blonde hair slipped across his face as he waved his arms and shook his head. Both he and John were speculating on the whereabouts of the bodies of the missing crew, echoing the thoughts and fears of many in the village. Joe hollered above the chatter and din.

'The thing is lads, we spent most of the day combing the bay and beaches and not a sign of anything. Usually by now there'd be at least one body washed ashore. Something's not right.'

John was quick to respond, while Phil looked on agitated.

'What's not right? When was the last time we had a storm as bad as this? Chances are the current has got them and swept them out to sea. They'll turn up on some beach up Alnmouth or Bamburgh way, if they haven't already.'

'So why haven't we heard?'

'Christ man Joe. It was only last night. There's time yet. Who's going to be out looking for them up there? They won't even know the ship's been wrecked yet. None of us can get out the village til this storm lifts.'

Joe become more animated, his arms flailing as he responded, pointing to somewhere far beyond the walls.

'Peggy went back up to Cresswell. Word will have got out. News travels fast, bad news even quicker. It'll be all up the coast by now. Folk will be looking. You'll get some buggers out hoping to get their hands on some of the cargo.'

John took a gulp of ale and waved his glass at Joe.

'Well then. Let's bide our time. What do you reckon Phil?'

Phil took a deep draw on his pipe and blew a huge puff of smoke into the air. He'd listened to all that was said, and as ever took his time before speaking.

'I reckon John's right Joe. We wait and the bodies will turn up. I can't see what you're angling at with all this something's not right talk. It doesn't do any good.'

Joe took a long drink and leant back against the wall behind the bench.

'What about this girl then?'

A scowl spread across Phil's face as he flung a cold stare at Joe.

'What about her?'

Joe replied, his usual impetuous lack of judgement worsened by the drink.

'Well my missus reckons there's some strange goings on there. All the street's talking. I mean, a young girl gets washed ashore. She's the only one that turns up, and survives the freezing sea and a night on the beach. Come on Phil. You must have asked yourself a few questions.'

Phil looked at the others. John was anxious, uneasy about his friend's response. Phil was a calm man, but he had a line, and once crossed he was not someone to meddle with. Jack stared into his pint glass. Phil was patient, tried to calm the simmering anger inside.

'I'll not deny it's strange, but it is what it is. She was there, she survived, and she's lucky I found her when I did. End of. All this idle chatter does no-one any good.'

Joe kept at it.

'Is it right she was naked when you found her?'

There was a pause while Phil played with his glass, the others looking on, waiting.

'Aye. It's true.'

'Well then see. I mean how...'

Phil butted in. His booming voice crushing Joe's words, as he fell back against the wall in shock and fear.

'Look she hasn't spoken yet so I still don't know the story of how she got there. All I know is she's a frightened young girl who has been through a bloody terrifying ordeal. She almost dies and then wakes up all alone in a strange place. She's probably lost all the people she was travelling with, maybe friends and relatives. Christ knows what she's feeling. Imagine yourself in that position Joe. How would you feel? I think we owe her a bit of time, don't you? Tell your poisonous gossips to bide their tongues or they'll have me to answer to.'

John looked at Joe, an expression telling him to leave it be. But Joe was ever one to have the final word.

'Aye you're right Phil. The poor lass. We'll find out soon enough. Let's just get on with our pints and be done with it for now.'

Joe should have left it there, but didn't. Instead he spoke again. One more final word, as they all feared he would, as he always did.

'Aye, give her time, but I still think there's something funny with it all.'

Phil hammered his fists onto the table as he launched himself to his feet. Glasses tumbled and shattered onto the floor as his huge frame towered over the three men. He leant towards Joe, his head edging closer to the younger man's face. The thick bristles of Phil's beard were almost touching Joe who could smell the cocktail of tobacco and ale on Phil's breath. As he stood over him the voice lowered, the words still slow and forceful, making no mistake as to their meaning and intent.

'Leave it Joe! Do you hear me? Tell your missus and all the others to keep their cackling to themselves. There's a young girl who survived and a lot more who didn't. Tell them to save their words, pray for their lost souls and thank God for the one we still have. That's all that matters here.'

Joe's face was locked in fear, his voice trembling. The young man had great respect for Phil, as they all did. He knew when Phil was wounded and the line had been crossed.

'Phil I'm sorry mate. It's the drink talking. You know what I'm like. Here, let me get another round in.'

'Nah. I'm done for the night. Catch you later lads.'

Phil pushed the table aside, stormed across the bar and left. Heading into the storm, he began the short walk up the main street towards home. The others stayed for a few more drinks they would regret, then made their way along the same route. The night was pitch black with only the occasional hazy light from a gas lamp to guide their way. At the top of the main street they entered the narrow lanes of the fisher end of the village. John then Jack bid their good nights as they reached their homes where a roaring fire and sharp words awaited. Joe lived at the bottom of the lane near the quay wall and lifeboat station. He stumbled alone down the lane, meandering in a snaking path, muttering to himself. Nearing the end of the lane Joe stopped as something caught his eye. At first he thought it was the hazy light and shadows playing tricks. Rubbing his eyes, Joe shuffled forward, creeping closer, slowing as he neared.

By the rear door of the lifeboat station, just beyond the darkest shadows, there was a girl. She had long black hair matching an ornate gown which flowed to her feet. Her face and body gave off the faintest glow, a shimmering aura emanating from pale, translucent skin. She said nothing, as her eyes locked on Joe, a gaze soft and inviting. Lifting her arm, the girl pointed at Joe and beckoned him. Joe shook his head and looked around him. They were alone, only the howling swirl of wind and rain could be heard. The girl smiled and continued to urge Joe forward. Without knowing or even wanting to the young man felt himself moving towards her. All the while her hand and eyes were drawing him in. Soon Joe was upon her, the dark eyes just below his, gazing up, pleading. Her face was perfect, sculpted in delicate porcelain. She looked down at Joe's lips, then back to his eyes. Something took over and Joe felt himself leaning into her, their lips touching. A cold shiver ran through him, as he tasted her breath. It was either fire or ice, so cold it burned his throat. Eyes closed and Joe's mind emptied as the girl turned, took him by the hand, and led him step by step down the jetty and across the sand. The wind continued to wail around them sweeping through her hair, tossing and turning, dancing with the needles of lashing rain.

As they tiptoed across the beach a sound could be heard from the darkness of the sea. It was the gentle sound of wailing, a beautiful, hypnotic sound, as though the sea itself was crying. They continued, step by step, two shadows gliding across the sand. They reached the edge of the waves as they smashed against the shore. The girl kept walking without pause into the churning waters. She still held Joe's hand, guiding him into the icy shallows. His eyes were still closed, his mind blank, lost. Soon the arctic water leapt past their middle, but the girl kept on pushing ahead, step by step, as the waves lifted her majestic gown. There was a pause, then she dived headfirst into the frozen sea. Without hesitation Joe followed. As they disappeared beneath the tumbling waves the cry of the sea continued to echo across the night sky, dampened by the wall of cloud, the wind and the rain.

The Storm

It stopped, as soon as it began. All that remained was the storm.

....

Phil lay asleep in the chair by the fire, his snoring loud enough to wake the street. Mary was clearing the table, and as she shuffled past every now and then would give him a kick. He would wake with a jolt then slip back into drunken slumber and the snoring would return. Ella sat in her chair as usual, arms folded across her stomach, staring into the heart of the fire, lost in thought. Behind the thin curtain in the corner the young girl was sleeping. She had lain there since late afternoon, never stirring, not a sound other than the gentle purr of breathing. Mary finished up the last of the plates and sat in the armchair closest to Ella. She gazed at the old woman, whose eyes never left the flickering light of the flames. Mary leant forward and whispered.

'Is everything OK nan? You're quiet, tonight.'

Ella lifted her eyes from the fire and sighed. She looked to the corner at the curtain concealing the bed and sat upright in the chair. Edging forward towards Mary, Ella replied, her voice quiet, though the gravel still rattled in her throat.

'We need to be careful Mary.'

Mary looked puzzled as Ella continued.

'The girl. She doesn't belong here. She needs to go back to where she came from.'

Mary frowned and leant in further.

'I know this isn't easy for any of us. We haven't got the room, and things have been difficult these past few months.'

Mary paused and cleared her throat before continuing.

'But think of what the poor girl has been through. She must be terrified, bless her. We can't do anything till the storm lifts and then Phil will make sure the folk at Morpeth get her home.'

'I know you think I'm just an old moaner and set in my ways, but believe me this is more serious than that. I'm only saying it for the good of us all. Nothing good can come of this.'

There was an eery silence as Mary and Ella's eyes locked. Mary could see the concern in Ella's face. The cold mask had lifted and there was a tenderness, a pleading. Both were silent, as Mary churned over her nan's words. Ella continued, her voice still no more than a whisper.

'I've seen this before Mary. Seen the like's of her before. Her kind. You need to get rid of her quickly or there'll be tragedy. Mark my words. When they come, it always ends in tears.'

The old woman's voice cracked and the whisper faded to nothing. Mary shook her head and placed her hand on Ella's. Tears began to form in Ella's eyes, small beads of water, just enough to glisten in the candlelight, too stubborn to break free. Mary squeezed her nan's hand.

'Please nan. Don't make this any harder than it need be. We've all been through a lot. You know how difficult it's been, especially for Phil. This is important to him. We need to stick together.'

Mary looked down at the floor. Ella's hands were cold, her skin wrinkled and tough enveloping bony fingers of little flesh. The old woman reached out, lifted Mary's chin, looked her in the eye. There was something in the look, something Mary had never seen before. Ella cleared her throat and whispered once more.

'That's why I'm warning you. For you and for Phil. Please get rid of her Mary.'

Ella pulled her hand away and sat back in her chair, returning her gaze to the dancing flames. Mary looked on, waiting, lost for words, shifting her stare to the corner of the room, to the curtain, pondering what lay beyond. Quiet, sleeping, harmless, the lost young girl who had clung to life in the face of certain death. Phil had saved her, brought her back from the brink. She was a terrified creature in a strange world who had suffered and lost so much. A delicate soul who needed nothing but love and support. Mary felt her sorrow dissolve as the confusion and disappointment grew. Mary couldn't understand why Ella was acting this way. Mary had seen the cold bitterness and sharp tongue before, but even for the old woman this was unusual. There was something Ella wasn't saying, something she seemed to know.

Mary looked across at Phil, his gentle face lit by the warm glow. She thought of the piece that was now missing, the pain that never went away. Mary loved her nan, trusted and respected her, yet Mary's loyalty would always be with Phil. Despite everything that had happened, Phil was her husband, and this was as it should be, the oath she had made. Mary sat back in the chair, and let her mind drift, slipping into the warm comfort of sleep. Soon the whole house was draped in slumber. The minutes crept by, and the yellow flames died to orange embers. Candles flickered on, while others burnt out, the light disappearing with a fizz and a tiny thread of smoke. The room was wrapped in a blanket of calm while outside the storm raged on.

There was a hammering at the door, and they all sat up with a start. Each was still wandering in a world of dreams, not quite sure whether the banging was real. Mary was the first to shake off the haze, jumping to her feet and moving towards the door. A cold blast of air and icy rain burst through the crack as she opened it. A young woman poked through, her head wrapped in a navy shawl, face weathered and worried red.

'Can I come in Mary? It's Joe!'

'Of course Maggie.'

Mary stepped aside and ushered the young woman in. Taking the guest's wet shawl, Mary gestured to the armchair she had left empty. Ella rubbed her eyes, a frown still etched on her face, while Phil sat up leaning forward as Maggie took a seat. The visitor's dark hair was tied up in a bun, her face flush with the ravages of the storm. Maggie spoke, her voice high-pitched, frantic, often cracking, close to breaking down in tears.

'It's Joe. He hasn't come home. John and Jack said they left him hours ago. He was heading home. They're out looking for him now. He should have been home by now.'

Mary looked across at Phil, who was now on his feet pacing back and forth in front of the fire. He spoke.

'So John and Jack saw him last and no-one else after that?'

'No. Not that I know of. The thing is Phil...'

There was a pause as she fumbled with her words. Mary and Ella looked on urging her to speak, as Maggie squeezed out the words.

'I don't want you to take this the wrong way, but Jack mentioned that you and Joe had some sort of argument in the bar.'

Maggie stopped and looked around the room. She continued in a raised whisper.

'Something about the girl. Jack said you stormed off.'

Maggie paused and Phil stopped his pacing. He turned and looked down at Maggie, then around at the others. All eyes were on him, waiting for a response. Mary glared at her husband.

'Hang on a second. It wasn't a fight! We exchanged a few words that's all, and yes, I was angry. That's why I left but I came straight back here. Anyway what are you getting at Maggie?'

'Sorry Phil. I don't want you to think I'm coming here making accusations. I just thought you might have seen him after he left the others.'

Maggie lowered her head, struggling to fight back the tears. Mary knelt by the chair, wrapping an arm across Maggie's shoulder. Phil remained standing by the fire, towering over them as he replied.

'No Maggie I haven't. I came straight home, had some supper, then fell asleep in the chair. The last I saw of Joe was in the bar.'

Mary looked up at Phil.

'It's true Maggie. Phil's been here with us for hours.'

Mary scowled at Phil, but lowered her voice.

'Why were you fighting about the girl?'

'I told you we weren't fighting. We just had a few words. Yes it got a bit heated, but it was nothing. Joe said some things about the girl and I put him right that's all. It was drunken talk. Christ, there's been a lot worse said. I left cos I was tired. It's been a tough few days.'

Phil caught Mary's stare, hoping she would let it drop. Mary kept pressing, her face making no attempt to disguise the festering anger.

'What things were said about the girl? I want to know.'

'I told you it was nothing. There's been some gossip and Joe let a few things out cos of the drink. People are bound to talk. Just leave it.'

Phil raised his eyebrows and nodded towards Maggie. Mary ignored him and continued to push.

'What kind of gossip?'

Mary shifted her eyes towards Maggie whose head was still lowered, staring at the floor. Maggie was sniffling, reluctant to get involved, pretending not to hear. Meanwhile, Phil was in no mood for an interrogation.

'Look I told you it was nothing, now for Christ's sake will you leave it!'

Phil's voice roared, as the others cowered.

It was quiet at first, soft but unmistakable. It came from behind the curtain, a slow, chilling wail. With each cry it got louder until it filled the whole room. Soon it was deafening, as Mary rushed over to the curtain. Pulling it back they saw the young girl sitting on the bed, arms wrapped around her knees, legs pulled in tight against her body. She was rocking back and forward, still screeching out the disturbing sound. The others looked on in shock as the girl continued to sway on the bed, eyes a vacant stare, weeping and wailing. Her lips were moving as if trying to form words, but only the sobbing and the cries came.

Maggie got to her feet and edged towards the bed where Phil was standing already. Mary reached down and touched the girl's shoulder. The girl ignored her, and continued to sway, letting out cry after cry, increasing in speed and intensity all the while. The wailing built to a blood-curdling crescendo, then stopped with a jolt as she passed out and flopped onto the bed. Soaking in sweat, eyelids open, her jet black eyes were empty, staring into the nowhere beyond. Mary felt the girl's forehead, then wrist and looked back at Maggie and Phil. Horror swept across Mary's face as she looked behind them towards the door. It was open, as the storm howled outside, and rain poured in. Phil stared down at Ella's chair. It was empty. The old woman had gone.

6

Phil snaked through the lanes down towards the lifeboat station, guided only by the old lantern in his hand. He struggled for breath as his legs heaved his body forward. The light from the lantern glistened against the wet and shiny cobble stones. The roar of the waves grew louder as he approached the quay wall. The cottages were silent, an occasional light glimmering through a window. The streets were deserted, the crunch of Phil's boots the only sign of life.

Reaching the bottom of the lane Phil heard someone calling from behind. It was a woman's voice, a familiar one. The voice drifted louder and softer as it swirled in the wind. He turned to see John's wife running towards him, shuffling in an oversized dress, a look of relief and exhaustion on her face. Her short, stout frame was dwarfed against his large shadow, but she knew Phil well, had played with him as a child, had seen him whimper at the sight of blood. They had grown like sister and brother.

'Phil, it's Ella. She's at our place. Don't worry, she's fine, but I think you need to speak with her. She's in a rage, cursing, saying she won't go back to the house. It's something about the girl. What's happened?'

'Thanks Beth. She's just being a daft old bugger, as usual. There's been a bit of drama at our place. The girl got upset and was screaming a bit. She's traumatised. It's understandable after what she's been through. The poor lass probably doesn't know what's happening. Ella was a bit spooked by it. You know what some of these old folk can be like, and you know Ella better than anyone. She reads too much into these things.'

Beth gave him an awkward look, as the lantern cast an eery glow on both their faces. Beth did know Ella, but she also knew Phil. She replied.

'You'll have a job on your hands convincing her to come home. She sounds determined and Ella isn't one to budge easily.'

They both exchanged awkward looks.

'I don't mind if she stays with us, at least until you get things sorted with the girl.'

'That'd be a big help. It isn't going to work with Ella and the girl under the same roof. She doesn't take kindly to strangers at the best of times. It'll only be for a couple of days at the most till the storm lifts. As soon as it clears I'll take the girl to Morpeth and they'll get her home.'

Beth nodded.

'It's no trouble Phil. I best hide the gin though.'

Phil shook his head and laughed, all the while twirling his fingers through his beard. Beth spoke.

'Any sign of Joe yet?'

'No, not that I know of. I've only just found out he's missing. Do you know whereabouts John went looking for him?'

'He said he'd look along the bay and head towards the Eye. Though I'm not sure why Joe would head out there in this weather.'

Phil shook his head, and looked into the distance to the far side of the bay. The blackness of the night and wall of rain meant only the faintest outline of a shadow could be seen. The shadow of the Eye was unmistakable to all in the village, a hole in the cliff face that looked out across the bay. Phil looked back at Beth, caught the air of discomfort in her expression, of something known, but not said. He spoke.

'He was pretty tanked up, and you know Joe. He doesn't hold back when he's had a few. We had a rough night, last night. The rescue got to us all, especially the young lads.'

Phil paused.

'I shouldn't have taken them.'

Beth reached out and touched Phil's arm. Lowering his head, gazing at the ground he continued. His voice softer, a mumble, as though he were speaking to himself not Beth.

'I think he wanted to let off some steam. Maybe once the sea air hit him the drink got the better of him. We've all seen it happen. He can't take his drink at the best of times.'

Beth frowned and gripped Phil's arm. He continued to stare downward, avoiding her sympathetic gaze. There was a long silence before Beth spoke.

'Is it true you and Joe had a row about the girl?'

Phil looked up.

'For Christ's sake Beth. Not you as well. We had a few words that was all. It was nothing. Now the bloke's gone missing and…I mean he's a mate.'

Phil glared at Beth, her diminutive frame shrinking even more.

'Sorry Phil. I'm not saying you had anything to do with it. I just thought if he was upset cos of the row he might have gone off somewhere to talk about it with someone. You know there are others Joe is very close to.'

They exchanged knowing looks as Beth continued.

'Have you tried some of the places he might have gone. Like you say he was drunk. He may have paid someone a visit.'

Phil knew what Beth meant, and it was something he should have thought of. Something they dare not mention in front of Maggie. Phil spoke.

'If he'd gone there he'd be back by now. Do you think Maggie knows?'

'I don't know. She'd be a fool not to. But sometimes you pretend. We all do. She knew what he was like when they married, and let's face it most of the village seem to know what's going on. If he's there I hope someone gives him a good hiding when they find him. The selfish bastard.'

Beth took Phil's hand as rain ran down her face. She struggled with her other hand to keep the shawl around her head, as the wind fought with her.

'Chances are he's with her. Don't worry. He'll turn up. They always do eventually.'

Phil smiled at her. Beth had always been Phil's other love, a different kind of love, a familiar love, of shared childhoods and memories. If it hadn't been for Mary who knows. Beth was a good woman, loyal and kind. Like Mary, just not her. There was only ever one love like Mary. Unlike his wife, Beth was a straight talker, held nothing back, always spoke her mind, sometimes without thinking it through. Neither woman had enemies, such was their grace and charm and the respect they commanded within the village. Phil felt the soft touch of Beth's tiny, delicate fingers in his huge gnarled hands. Her skin was warm and soft. His throat and lips were dry, and he struggled to form the words.

'There's no harm done Beth. It's been a long day, and we're all exhausted. This storm is getting to us all.'

They both looked up at the sky, felt a blast of the wind and rain. They were used to weather, had seen it all in their time, but there was something different about this storm. Neither of them could explain it, but they sensed it. Phil took his hat off and shook it.

'Look Beth I best be heading off. I'll see if I can find John and that sod Joe. When I do he's going to regret it. I'll head out towards the Eye. Will you go and tell Mary that Ella's at your place? She'll be worried sick, but didn't want to leave the girl.'

Beth nodded, stood on her toes and hugged Phil. She stretched to wrap her arms around him. Phil leant forward and embraced her, lifting her from the ground like a doll. As they both let go Beth stepped back and wiped the rain from her eyes.

'I'll go and tell Mary. You go and find those two, and take care. Make sure you all get back safe now.'

Beth headed back up the lane as Phil crossed the beach and made his way along the bay. Shuffling towards the waterline, his shadow hugged the firm sand left by the receding tide. He was careful not to stray too close to the waves, as they continued to batter the beach. The night had added another layer of bite to the arctic weather. The lantern provided the only light, but no warmth. As he pushed on, his legs felt heavier with every step, the wind and rain sucking the last drops of energy from aching limbs.

The Eye was a narrow outcrop of rock reaching out to sea marking the end of the long arc of the bay. It took its name from the large hole in the centre of the rock, high enough to walk through, and noticeable from a distance, giving a distinctive look. On the far side of the Eye was a small burn which separated the village from the cliffs. Fields stretched beyond towards the nearby mining community. A crumbling wooden bridge crossed the burn. Few ventured over the bridge, but as a child Phil would often explore the fields, cliffs and beaches beyond.

The shadow of the Eye neared, and soon Phil was scrambling over the slippery rocks, lined with seaweed and dotted with deep pools. He and his friends came here as kids, spending hours searching for the crabs that hid under stones, and catching minnows trapped by the receding tide. This was where sea and life began for him, before he ever ventured out on his father's boat. Fishing was in his blood, all he ever felt the urge to do. The sea was all he ever knew. It seduced him, gave him a life, but took his father and many others that he knew.

Dragging himself up the edge of the rocks Phil clambered through the Eye. The wind intensified as it shot through the hole. Even with his strength Phil had to push hard to get through as the gusts forced him back, swaying on his tired and unsteady feet. He leant against the rocks, desperate for a rest, body bent over, hands resting on his thighs, the lantern at his feet. He heaved as his lungs burned with every gasp of air.

A strange sensation swept over him, the feeling that of being watched. Grabbing the lantern Phil lifted it in front of him, and the dim orange glow of light caught her face. Just a few feet away, she was staring at him. It was her, he would know her anywhere, just as it had been before she went away. Lifeless eyes with tears running onto white delicate cheeks. She was dressed in black, the same clothes on the day she went missing. Her shoulders were draped in dark strands of her hair. Phil looked down her body and could see she was drenched and dripping water, more than mere rainwater. It was pouring from her, leaving a puddle at her feet. Her face was cold without emotion, her eyes burning into him. Phil struggled to speak, his voice cracked and faltering.

'I thought you'd gone. What do you want?'

There was no reply.

'Look I don't know what you want from me! I've said sorry. How long do you want to keep punishing me like this?'

Silence, as her piercing eyes glowed in the haze of the flickering light of the lantern.

'There isn't a day goes by without me thinking about what happened. If you want me to suffer, believe me I do, every day. Tell me. What do I have to do for your forgiveness? Tell me, or just leave me be!'

Her penetrating stare reached deep inside his head. His mind was burning, desperate for her to let go. Phil lunged forward to grab her but clutched at air, faltering on his feet, and stumbling onto the rocks. She was gone. Phil lifted himself to his feet, swung round, thrusting the lantern forward to see if she was still there, hiding in the shadows. There was no-one. For a moment the crashing cacophony of the storm subsided. It was as though the waves, wind, and rain had disappeared. All he heard was a muffled voice, sailing through the air, drifting in and out of earshot, becoming clearer as it neared. Straining his eyes, reaching out into the depths of the darkness, Phil saw the faintest flicker of light moving towards him. There was a shadow alongside it. Then he heard a voice.

'Phil? Is that you? Phil?'

Shaking himself from the haze, Phil realised who it was.

'Over here John. It's me.'

Phil lifted the lantern high above his head, as his friend approached, frozen and soaked through. Phil spoke.

'Any sign of Joe?'

'No. It was always a longshot. I doubt even he would be daft enough to come out here in this.'

The silence had gone now, the full orchestra of the storm played out above their heads.

'Did you get to go to the house and speak to her?'

'Aye. She was in, though her old fella wasn't happy at me knocking them up at this time. She swears she hasn't seen him. She's telling the truth. I could see she was shocked when I told her why. She'll have a few more questions to answer tonight though.'

Phil frowned. The light on his lantern dipped. For a moment it threatened to go out, but it fizzed back into life again.

'So what now?'

John stared at Phil, a worried look on his face.

'It's more complicated than that.'

'What do you mean, more complicated?'

John put his head down.

'She's with child.'

Phil lowered the lantern, as he thought on the words, trying to process their meaning.

'So her and Maggie. Christ. Did Joe know?'

John lifted his head and nodded.

'Apparently, she told him yesterday.'

The possibilities were hurtling through Phil's mind, too many for him to take. Both men stood silent for a while, locked deep in thought. John was the first to speak.

'There's no way you think he'd do something stupid.'

'No! Not Joe. I just can't see it.'

Phil said the words, but the thought had crossed his mind. He continued.

'If he'd a lot on his plate and too much to drink he might have gone off somewhere to clear his head. Something might have happened on the way. He could have fallen. You know what it's like when you're drunk. Knowing Joe he'll be having a kip somewhere.'

'Aye, but where? If he's fallen he won't last long tonight.'

Both men exchanged worried stares, as Phil turned and moved out of the scant shelter of the Eye. He stumbled towards the edge of the rocky embankment, and looked out over the shadow of the rocks. Turning back, Phil gestured to John.

'Come on. Let's head back to the station. We'll round up a few more folk and organise a search. We need to make sure we cover as much as we can and quickly.'

The two men hurried back along the bay towards the station. They were facing another long night ahead, a night of more peril and uncertainty, more heartache within the menacing eye of the storm.

....

Mary looked on as Maggie wiped her eyes. Both sat at the table in Beth and John's cottage. Beth was busy making another pot of tea while Ella sat by the fire. Mary placed her arm around Maggie and pulled her in tight.

'Don't worry. He'll turn up. Half the village is out looking for him.'

Mary could feel the trembling of Maggie's body as she continued to whimper and sob. Maggie dabbed the handkerchief on her eyes, while her other hand stroked her bulging stomach. Mary whispered in her ear.

'I'll need to be getting back to my place soon. I've left the girl sleeping, but I'm not sure how long she'll be settled for. I don't want her waking up on her own. You're welcome to come back with me.'

Maggie sat back and gazed at Mary through her tears.

'No. I mean, thanks Mary, but I think I'd rather stay here.'

There was an awkwardness to the response, and Mary suspected why. Reaching out, Mary hugged her again.

'It's OK. I understand.'

They sat for a while, Maggie's head resting on Mary's chest, moving up and down with the gentle movement of her breathing. Mary closed her eyes, trying to clear her mind. The tension of the evening was getting to her. While she struggled to keep a veneer of composure and calm, inside strong feelings were churning. For a moment the chaos subsided, replaced with the hum of family life. Mary focused on the sounds. There was the crackle of the fire and the clatter of cups in the corner. Beyond a veil in the other corner the muffled sound of children's voices could be heard. Sarah, the elder of Beth's children was telling Susan a night time story. Both had been woken by the commotion of Ella's arrival and the stream of visitors following Joe's disappearance. The children spoke in the whispers of the young, but Mary could hear every word. Susan spoke first in a playful, high pitched voice.

'So what's this story about Sarah?'

Sarah answered, her voice mellow and controlled, but still drifting across the room for all to hear who wanted to.

'It's about a girl who came from the sea.'

'How did she come from the sea? Did she live there?'

'Yes. She wasn't a real girl. She was a sea creature. She was a...'

The girl paused, as her sister responded.

'She was what? Tell me.'

'I'm not allowed to say cos it's bad luck.'

Mary opened her eyes and sat up, shuffling in the chair. Maggie's head was still pressed against her chest, and she continued her quiet sobbing. Mary's mind was focused on something else now, the girls. Susan's voice cut through the room again.

'Why's it bad luck?'

'I don't know. Auntie Ella told me.'

'So why does the girl come from the sea?'

There was a long moment of silence. Mary looked across at Ella and Beth. Both were looking in the direction of the corner, listening beyond the curtain. Beth caught Mary's eye and looked away as Sarah answered her sister.

'She comes to take our men.'

'Why?'

'Because she wants to have babies with them.'

The sound of giggling echoed through the room as Susan replied in a giddy voice.

'Uurrrgh. Tell me a different story. I don't like that one, it's scary.'

Sarah's voice was faltering, but her response was louder and clearer than ever.

The Storm

'It is scary, but Auntie Ella says these stories are important. We have to learn them and pass them on.'

'Why?'

'So we learn to protect ourselves.'

Susan waited a moment before she spoke.

'Why do we need to protect ourselves.'

'From them, the strangers, the people that come to harm us.'

Ella stared at Mary, frowned then looked away, back into the heart of the roaring flames. Mary felt the weight of Maggie's head lift from her chest as she sat up. Wiping away her tears with the handkerchief she gazed at Mary with a frown. Meanwhile Beth ran over to the corner and dipped in behind the veil. Beth spoke.

'Time to go to sleep girls. Story time is over.'

Susan protested, close to tears.

'But mum I was only saying what Auntie Ella told me.'

'No buts. It's late and you both need to sleep now. Do you hear me? No arguments. Auntie Ella shouldn't be telling you such stories. Now forget them and go to sleep.'

Beth returned from behind the veil, and glanced at Mary and Maggie. She then thrust a cold look of anger at Ella who remained transfixed on the fire. The air was thick with tension now, mixed with the overpowering heat of the fire. Maggie gave Mary a quizzical look, but Mary was in no mood to chat. There were other things on her mind. Mary got to her feet and moved round by the fire, lowering her face towards Ella. She paused for a moment, thinking through what she wanted to say. Mary took a breath and began to growl the words at her nan, spitting them at her in a calm, menacing tone.

'You see nan. This is how it all starts. The fear, the suspicion, the hatred. You're poisoning the girl's minds with your superstition.

Mary paused, waiting for a response, but Ella sat stone faced as ever, refusing to even catch her granddaughter's eye. Mary continued.

'You can be a bitter, twisted old fool at times.'

Standing upright, Mary pulled her shawl in tight, nodded to the others and made for the door. Stepping out into the cruel night, she marched down the street fighting with the relentless wind and rain. Streams of water cascaded across the cobblestones, weaving their way to the bottom of the lane. Mary ploughed through the puddles and disappeared into the shadows of the night.

Back in Beth's house the two girls lay under the sheets, the rain rattling against the window. Sarah was still whispering the story to her sister who lay trembling with terror. The story of a strange, beautiful creature who arrived in the village one day. She came from the sea, to mesmerise and seduce the men. She came to steal them, lay with them, and bear their children. These were not ordinary children, but the children of the sea. It was an ancient story, older than the village itself. A tale that had been passed down through generation after generation. A story that had evolved, one that always had the same beginning, but many different endings.

7

'Any news?'

Mary helped Phil take off his wet clothes and passed him a towel.

'Nothing.'

'There's a cup of tea on the table and a fresh night gown on the chair.'

Phil got dressed and sat by the fire, sipping the hot tea, feeling the comfort and reassurance as it slid down his throat burning his chest. He gazed into the heart of the flames as they leapt towards the chimney, grasping, always just out of reach. Every now and then there would be a loud crack as the fire caught a piece of stone and spat it onto the rug. Reaching down Phil flicked the burning ember onto the hearth and flopped back into the chair, heaving under his weight. Mary busied herself in the kitchen area. There was little to do that she hadn't done a hundred times already that night, but she wanted to give Phil time. He would speak when ready, first he needed to come to terms with the night. Phil finished his tea and placed the mug by the side of the chair. There was a long silence neither wanted to break. Eventually, Mary spoke.

'Do you want anything to eat?'

'Is there any cheese and ham?'

Mary nodded. She began to cut large slices off the remainder of the bread, and laid them alongside pieces of cheese and ham on a plate. Dabbing a few spoonfuls of mustard by the side, she poured another mug of tea and placed them by her husband, then sat at the table. Mary watched as Phil wrapped the cheese and ham in the bread and smeared it in the mustard.

Crumbs clung to the bristles smothering his lips, as he munched away, washing each mouthful down with huge swigs of tea. Phil played with his beard and gazed into the fire. A thick blanket of tiredness was beginning to slip over him, his eyes became heavy and he drifted in and out of half sleep. Just as his head nodded forward and his mind plunged through the gateway of dreams and nightmares, Phil would see her face and wake with a start. Again and again the pattern repeated, the same image returning each time. Until his eyes closed, breathing changed and the snoring began. Mary looked on and smiled. Suddenly, Phil jumped up, with a look of horror and confusion. Mary was flung back in the chair, as her husband's eyes looked around the room, searching, still gripped with sleep and terror. Mary spoke.

'Are you OK?'

'What? What?'

Phil began to realise where he was, as he saw his wife's face. Rubbing his eyes he shook his head and gestured at Mary to move away.

'I'm fine. Don't fuss. I just got a bit of a fright that's all.'

'What's wrong?'

Phil pushed himself up in the chair.

'Nothing. It's been a long night. These past couple of days have been…'

His voice cracked. There was a long pause. Mary eased forward and spoke.

'A lot has happened.'

Mary pulled her chair closer to her husband.

'Try and get some rest Phil. Hopefully, this storm will lift and Joe will turn up.'

The Storm

Mary waited, gazing at her husband who stared into the fire, not wanting to look at her. Phil replied, still caressing his beard, his voice soft and fragile.

'There's something odd about Joe's disappearance. I've got a bad feeling about it.'

Silence enveloped the room again, only punctured by the whistle of the wind and crackle of the fire. Phil continued to gaze into the fire, not noticing the tear creeping from the corner of his wife's eye. Mary lowered her head, as Phil looked up and spoke.

'Did you manage to see Ella?'

'I did. I went over to Beth's earlier once the girl settled.'

'How was she?'

There was a pause. Mary sat back in the chair, still avoiding her husband's gaze. Phil shifted his eyes to the flames, then back to his wife, as he shuffled in the armchair. Phil spoke.

'What's wrong?'

Mary forced out the words, her voice no more than the softest whisper.

'Ella's been talking about the girl.'

Phil frowned, a worried look etched on his face.

'What's she been saying?'

'Just some superstitious nonsense. You know what folk are like. They see what they want to see, and I think with everything that's going on.'

Mary paused then continued.

'There are lots of questions and people are filling in the blanks.'

Phil was wide awake now, all remnants of tiredness smothered by the adrenalin of the anger churning inside.

'What sort of things?'

Mary sat upright, her hands clasped together, her fingers fidgeting.

'It's nothing Phil. Don't bother yourself with it.'

Phil's voice rose, struggling to contain his growing emotion.

'Tell me.'

Mary caught Phil's eye, and returned her stare to the floor.

'They're just the old stories. You know, about the dark haired girl who arrives from the sea, then…'

Mary's throat dried up. She coughed to clear it before continuing.

'The men start to disappear. You know the story they told us when we were kids.'

Phil nodded as his mind drifted back to some distant memory. He shook his head.

'I know the one. Nan used to tell us it as a bedtime story all the time.'

Phil snarled and thrust his head into his hands. Mary looked on, her face torn with worry and confusion, not knowing whether to reach out and comfort him. Phil lifted his head and spoke.

'There are folk round here that make my blood boil sometimes. What with their tongues wagging, and their stupid stories. It was the same after the accident. I spent weeks having to avoid the stares, or put folk right. Rubbish and gossip. Sticking their noses into other people's business.'

Phil pressed his fists against his forward and shook his head. Mary waited, looking for the right moment. After a while, she spoke in a gentle, reassuring whisper.

'They mean no harm Phil. You know that. People think the world of you round here, but they get scared. No-one knows what's going on, and even the best of folk behave differently.'

Mary took a moment to compose herself, as a spark leapt out of the fire and onto the rug. Phil leant forward without thinking and flicked the glowing fragment of stone onto the hearth. Mary continued.

'I'll speak to Ella in the morning. I'll tell her the girl spoke in the night and said a few English words. I can say she told us she's from the Embla. Hopefully, that'll keep them quiet and put a stop to the gossip.'

Phil looked at Mary.

'Thanks'

Phil glanced across at the veil, then looked back at his wife. Edging forward in his seat he lowered his voice.

'Do you think we should take her out? I'm not sure it helps keeping her in here all the time. I was thinking about church in the morning. We could take her to the service. It might help if folk see her, see how scared she is. Maybe that'll stop the tongues wagging.'

Mary smiled.

'I think it's a great idea. I'll sort some things for her to wear in the morning. Now stop fretting and try to get some rest. Don't worry about Joe. I'm sure he'll turn up in the morning.'

Phil grinned.

'I hope you're right.'

For the briefest of moments all worry evaporated, and the tension lifted. It was as it had been before, a time they were both struggling to capture and recall. Mary got to her feet and busied herself again, gathering blankets, and snuffing out the candles. Phil's eyes returned to the flames, watching as they began to fade. Soon Mary was done, and the couple nestled into separate armchairs and drifted off to sleep. The orange glow from the dying embers cast the only light around the room. Shadows leapt and danced as the crackle and hiss of the fire mingled with the rumble of Phil's snoring and the howl of the wind. The storm raged on outside. The village lay silent, each locked inside their stone cells. Beyond the veil the girl lay on the bed, eyes open, gazing at the ceiling, one hand stroking her stomach.

8

'Are you sure it's safe?'

Jack said what they all wondered, all but Tom who knew the house and grounds well. He had planned this, knew about the empty house, had been here before, many times. Tom spoke.

'Come on. I'll show you where we'll sleep.'

Annie passed a candle to Mable and led them out of the passage along a narrow corridor. The flicker of the light danced against the walls casting long shadows as they moved. There were flashes of yellow on dark canvas revealing tall paintings of solemn men and women. Each was dressed in strange ceremonial clothing. The corridor was cold, the air thick with the heavy odour of damp. Outside was the muted howling of the wind. Tom sensed the tension of his friends.

'Don't worry, it's been empty for years.'

Mable replied.

'What if someone's watching it?'

'No-one's bothered, especially not at this time of night and in this weather. I've been here before and it was fine.'

Mable spoke.

'I think it's creepy.'

Tom laughed.

'Only if you let it spook you. There's something about the place. You'll see.'

They kept moving to the end of the passage where Tom led them into a cavernous hall dominated by a long open staircase. The glow continued to reveal an array of painted faces, their lifeless eyes flashing past as light and shadow played with the darkness. Mable moved towards one of the paintings. The candlelight thrust a warm circle on the canvas. Mable's long blonde hair was draped across her shoulders, still wet from the rain, as were her clothes. Her pale, blue eyes locked onto the picture, gazing at the face staring down at her. It was an old man with grey, thinning hair combed over on top. His face was dour and stern, eyes looking away at something to his right. Two long sideburns hugged his cheeks. He was dressed in black, all but his white shirt and the red patterned scarf around his neck. The painting must have been at least two metres tall and had the most prominent place in the hallway.

As Mable gazed at the painting, Jack and Annie came and stood at each shoulder. Annie was the tallest and oldest of the group. Her harsh, pointed features and jet black hair stood out against the lighter and softer features of both her friends. Despite their contrasting looks, they all wore the same dour clothes scraped together by mothers in desperation. They dressed in anything given, passed on, or altered.

Annie spoke, her voice calm, quiet, almost a whisper, as though the silence of the hall required respect or she feared someone was listening to her words.

'Who do you think it is?'

They surveyed the image as it towered above them. There was something in the eyes, a glimmer of fear, perhaps pain. Jack replied.

'He doesn't look very happy, whoever he is.'

Annie spoke.

'No-one ever smiles in these pictures, do they? You'd think their lives were so miserable, despite all that money.'

There was a pause as they continued to be mesmerised by the face on the painting. Annie broke the silence again.

'My dad used to say their money came from our suffering. He said most of them had never done a proper day's work in their lives. That's all these big old buildings are, just the rich mocking us while we live in boats on the beach. Look at where all the rich folk in the village live. They're looking down on us. It isn't fair.'

Mable spotted a label at the base of the painting. She moved closer and dipped the candle towards it. She could just make out the writing engraved in the brass plate.

'It says Matthew Ridley, the First Provincial Grand Master of Northumberland, 1734. That sounds like a very grand title.'

Tom nodded.

'He must have been rich to own this house.'

Annie continued.

'They're only interested in lining their own pockets. They pretend they care for us poor but they'd just as soon send you to the workhouse to work as a slave. They've done nowt for us since we lost my dad. If it wasn't for the other fisher folk we'd have been in the workhouse a long time ago.'

Mable looked at the man in the painting again. There was something in his eyes, a quiet pride, but also a sadness. She thought about the grandeur of the building, the riches he enjoyed, the privileges he had gained. He must have been important to gain such a title and position. Maybe he was only looking out for his family like everyone else, but these were different people with different values. They were nothing to her. Mable spoke.

'I wonder why he looks so sad?'

Annie stepped back.

'It's just what they do for these pictures. Mind the rich folk in the village always seem miserable. They never so much as say hello, and always tell us to stay clear of their prissy little kids. I bet it costs a fortune to have these paintings done.'

Tom nodded.

'Aye. They want to show off their wealth, how important they are. It's all a waste of good money if you ask me.'

Tom ushered the others through one of the doors and into a small room. There were a couple of large sofas, some old ornate rugs, and shelves lining the walls filled with books. Around the edges of the room were various pieces of antique furniture, a number with ornaments on, clocks, dishes, vases, and candlesticks. The centre piece of the room was a wide and open fireplace with a heavy white stone surround. Above it stood an imposing mirror with an intricately carved frame. Annie used her candle to light another on a side table, as Jack and Tom flopped onto one of the sofas. Annie began to rummage through the drawers of a desk, while Mable stood in front of the fireplace, admiring the mirror. Annie approached the fireplace and spoke.

'Don't get too comfy you lot. You can give me a hand to get a fire going first.'

Annie and Jack prepared the fire as Tom and Mable lit more candles and laid them across the hearth and on the mantelpiece. Tom sat crossed legged on the rug at the edge of the hearth, facing the growing flames. Every now and then he would lean his body in closer to watch the lights dancing. Wrapped in a blanket, Tom could still feel the cold icy air of the rest of the room on the back of his neck. Mable sat alongside. She said nothing, just listened to the rattle of the rain and the wind whistling through the windows and under the door. If they had known or looked closer they may have seen the shadow by the window, the silhouette of a girl, standing on the balcony, watching, waiting for her moment. Not now, but soon.

Mable reached out and touched Tom, stroking his hair. She did it without thinking. They had been courting for a few months. Both only fifteen, they figured life had little else to offer but each other. Tom was looking to find a place on a boat, determined to find work and make a difference for his family. Once he did, the future would be better. Life's cruelty had taught them to live for the moment, grab fun while they could.

Jack and Annie lay silent on the sofa, wrapped in each other's arms. They too were just a couple of kids whose lives had been destroyed by tragedy. Fate had taken what little they had, and they sought comfort in friendship and young love. As Jack and Annie slept, Mable and Tom lay on the rug in front of the fire, whispering and giggling, stealing hungry kisses. One by one they drifted off to sleep. Silence and darkness crept over the room, as the candles faded and died. Outside, in the howling night the shadow of the girl had disappeared. She was somewhere else, still watching and waiting. Her moment was approaching.

....

Tom woke and lit a few of the candles. The others were fast asleep, their faces lit by the gentle light. He gazed down at Mable as she lay, looking peaceful and content, a gentle smile on her face. Tom moved round and sat on a cushion by the hearth, his back against the wall facing into the room. The flames from the fire dissolved the shadows. Old paintings littered the walls, the long dead and forgotten. Row upon row of books filled shelves. Tom thought about the writers, where they might have lived, how their world differed. His father would tell him stories when he was a young boy, not from books, but those he had learned, old folk tales passed down through families. They were wild stories, usually involving young girls falling foul of a mythical creature or an evil local lord. Many of the stories were of the sea. They taught respect and fear.

The sea. The giver and taker of life. Tom's mother and father had been determined he would better himself, so they sent him to one of the elderly leaders for reading lessons. They also sent him to the church Sunday school, but he was thrown out for stealing and punching another boy. He was angry, not least because of the beating his father gave him, but he knew he deserved it. Tom loved books, but rarely got the chance to read. His family had only one book, a bible.

Tom got to his feet, picked up a candlestick, and moved to one of the shelves. He touched the books, tracing a line along them, glancing at the array of titles. One caught his eye. He pulled it from the grip of the others. They struggled and tugged as though reluctant to let it go. Tom wrestled the book free, and blew off the dust. 'Frankenstein by Mary Shelley.' Opening the cover, Tom picked a random page and squinting could just make out the dense words. 'Beware; for I am fearless, and therefore powerful.' He opened it at another page. 'There is something at work in my soul, which I do not understand.' One more, a final time. 'When falsehood can look so like the truth, who can assure themselves of certain happiness?'

The words struck Tom with their beauty. They were puzzling, mesmerising. He wondered what they meant as he closed the pages and placed the book back on the shelf. Tom glided around the room, studying the pictures, touching the objects. There was the sound of footsteps running in the hall, quiet but distinct, only lasting a moment. Tom listened, his hand trembling as he held the candlestick. Waiting, all he could hear was the rattle and howl of the storm above the sound of his quickening breathing. There was nothing. Maybe he had imagined it? He was tired. It had been a long day, and there was something about this building, something strange, the atmosphere, the energy. The house played tricks with his mind.

Tom moved back to the hearth, sat on the cushion, and gazed at Mable. He felt himself dozing, but fought hard to conquer it. His head bobbed this way and that, jerking back and forth with a jolt. His eyelids were heavy, his mind floating elsewhere. Something urged him to stay awake. The noise came from beyond the door. Tom sat up, his thoughts hazy, he couldn't be sure if it was real. He heard the sound again, no mistaking it this time. Footsteps, clear and definite and louder than before. Looking across at the others, Tom thought about waking them, but decided against it. He would see who it was alone.

Creeping to his feet, Tom took out a small pocket knife, lifted the candlestick and edged towards the door. Leaning his head against it, he waited, one hand clutching the knife, the other the candlestick. He listened, trying to soften his breathing, poised, ready to pounce. The sound came again, this time the steps were slower, less pronounced, creeping and shuffling, trying not to be heard. They were distant, but moving nearer, and with each one Tom sensed a subtle rise in their intensity. One by one, closer and closer, then they stopped, just outside the door. There was a long, ominous silence.

Tom struggled to breathe as he listened, reaching out behind the door, searching through the darkness for any fragments of movement or sound. There was nothing, not even the softness of breathing. The eye of his mind seeped into the corridor, trying to picture what lay beyond. Drawing on every sense, he struggled to build pieces of an image in his head. Tom could feel its presence. Something was there, waiting.

The rumble of the storm and pounding of Tom's heart were the only sounds. Easing the handle of the door, Tom teased it open. There was a creak as it moved. He stopped, listened, but there was nothing. Tom glanced back at the others, but no-one stirred. Peering through the narrow crack, the passage was pitch black. Edging the door open further, Tom lifted the candlestick towards the gap, throwing the faintest shaft of light out front. Stepping into the corridor Tom looked in both directions. The candle's weak glow revealed little. The passage was black, its furthest reaches cloaked in pure darkness. Shuffling to his right, with soft, delicate footsteps, the candlelight brushed away the shadows as Tom glided forward. The faint light unveiled bare wooden floorboards, the doors to other rooms, and more faded paintings. Faces on the walls looked down, still and lifeless, their eyes following him.

Around twenty paces along the passage, Tom paused. There was a fizz of burning wax accompanied by the steady rhythm of his breathing. His mind reached into the depths of the darkness ahead, searching for the presence. He sensed something, a shadow flashing across the corridor. There was another, this time caught by the flicker of the light. More movements. No sound, no footsteps, only a flurry of shadows, moving this way and that, darting across the dark edges of the corridor. Tom grabbed at them, trying to catch one. A shadow stopped dead centre just within reach of the candle's glow. Tom could see the presence now, a short, black silhouette of a figure, a girl. As Tom watched the shadow seemed to grow, becoming more imposing. Cloaking the whole of the corridor in a veil of darkness, it sucked out all the light, and snuffed out the flickering flame. The shadow loomed over Tom, hovering still and silent.

Tom rubbed his eyes, and she was there, standing before him, her cold breath brushing against his lips. Black hair flowed down a long, lavish dress. Her face gave out a hypnotic glow from the whitest porcelain skin. Dark eyes locked with his in silent duel. The girl leant forward and kissed him. Tom felt a bolt of the bitterest cold shoot through his body like shards of icy spears jabbing his heart. His mind was gripped in darkness as a blanket of swirling cloud swept through him. The girl took Tom by the hand and led him along the corridor and down the stairs. Opening the rear door, they stepped outside into the tyranny of the storm. Tom followed her, eyes closed, a dead smile on his face. The girl floated across the garden, Tom close behind, gliding down the steps and onto the beach below. The wind and rain continued their assault, battering them as they moved across the sand. Tom felt nothing, the girl crept on towards the waves.

A mesmerising chorus of singing drifted from the water. It was the sound of wailing, as if the sea were weeping. The girl and Tom tiptoed towards the waves and stepped into the water. The raging sea rolled and churned upon the beach, as the girl plunged forward into the waves, leading Tom behind her. A huge wall of water crashed over them and both were swallowed by the icy depths disappearing beneath the pounding waves. The weeping of the sea continued, long into the night, as the villagers lay locked in the deepest sleep. No-one heard the water's mournful cries. Back in the house, Mable tossed and turned on the rug in front of the fireplace, troubled by a disturbing dream, a strange enchanting music echoing throughout, a wailing pressing down, suffocating her. At dawn, when the first shafts of sunlight should have been making their way from behind the horizon, the cries of the sea ended. All that remained was the symphony of the storm.

DAY TWO

Chris Ord

9

The people huddled together in pairs and small groups, heads bowed, covered with hats and shawls. All wore their best clothes despite the weather. The rain had eased for a while, but the arctic wind still battered the village. The procession of villagers made their way across sand covered cobbles and grassy dunes onto the promenade. Trudging past the overturned boats, the makeshift village on the far end of the beach, they snaked up the slow incline and through the gates of the churchyard. The bell rang to summon them, a single repetitive toll echoing across the sky, fighting with the wind. The congregation slowed as they neared the narrow entrance, where a line of worshippers stood. Each waited to be greeted by the vicar, a few simple words of comfort and welcome, and grumblings about the weather. Other things were exchanged too, nods, winks, the occasional knowing gesture. In the mumblings of the crowd one topic dominated above all else.

Phil and Mary walked either side of the girl, almost carrying her as she stumbled along the short journey. The girl trembled and whimpered all the way, kept her head fixed on the ground, avoiding all stares and glances from those around her. Phil and Mary were met with several greetings, but many more querying eyes, and suspicious stares. Mary pressed Phil's arm, a gentle reminder to remain calm. As they approached the stone wall surrounding the churchyard an old lady and her granddaughter drew near. Kitty was an elder stateswoman of the fishing area of the village. Respected and feared by many, tolerated by others. Like her great friend Ella, she too had the weather beaten, sea and sun ravaged skin, and the brutal tongue to match. The old woman made it her business to know everything, presenting herself as a sage and confidante, open to sharing wisdom and advice, while only seeking news and gossip. Mary winced as she saw Kitty and the granddaughter approaching and squeezed Phil's side even harder. Kitty stopped, looking the girl up and down with disdain, then turned to Phil and Mary and spoke.

'Good morning. Now what do we have here? Is this the poor creature you found washed up on the beach Phillip?'

Mary nipped Phil in the side again and replied before her husband could.

'Good morning Kitty. Yes, it is.'

Kitty continued.

'Does she have a name?'

'I'm sure she does, but we don't know it. She's only said a few words. She's been through quite an ordeal and is still in shock. We just need to give her time.'

Kitty leant forward arching her body, pushing her face into the girl's line of sight. Meanwhile, the girl continued to stare at the floor, shivering and muttering in a whisper, letting out quiet, unsettling whimpers. Kitty spoke in a slow, condescending tone, as if she were addressing a young child.

'Listen to you, poor thing. You sound like a puppy dog. Do you understand what I'm saying girl? Do you speak any English?'

Mary felt Phil's body stiffen. Poking her husband in the side, she hurled a sharp stare at him, then spoke again before he could bite.

'I'm not sure she'll answer Kitty. She doesn't speak much English, but said a few words last night. We think she's from Norway, where the Embla was from.'

The Storm

Kitty looked the girl up and down, then shifted her cold stare to Phil and Mary. Dressed in a dark dress and wrapped in a knitted cardigan and shawl, she looked far more delicate and frail than her fiery tongue would suggest. Her age and air of weakness were the weapons she used to disarm opponents, but most in the village knew her well enough.

'They speak a funny language them foreigners, don't they? I've met a lot over the years passing through on the boats. You have to watch them as well. They have strange ways some of them. Can't be trusted. Norway you say? I've heard talk she may be from somewhere else. Let's hope it is Norway, for all our sakes.'

Phil could not bite his tongue any longer, despite the string of nips and jabs. He spoke, his voice controlled, but with sufficient volume and agitation to let Kitty know his true feelings.

'Like Mary said Kitty. The girl has been through a lot, the least we can do is show her some warmth and hospitality, and help her get back home. I'm sure she'll have loved ones somewhere who are worried sick. That's something we can all understand in any language, can't we?'

'I guess so Phillip. Let's hope you find that home and get her back there soon. That's what we all want to see, a quick ending to this, get things in the village back to normal.'

Kitty's granddaughter Liz, was still alongside clutching the old woman's arm. Liz was a plain girl who had lost her husband at sea and was left to care for their two small children. Faced with destitution, she had moved in with Kitty and the two fed off the bitterness and spite of the other. Any glimmer of joy and hope in Liz's young life had been stripped from her piece by piece, and Kitty made sure she would never find it again. Liz tugged at her nan's arm.

'Come on nan. Let's be going. We need to get you inside from this weather. It looks like the rain is coming back. Leave Mary, Phil and this poor creature be.'

Kitty yanked at Liz's arm as she tugged it, making it clear she was in no hurry to move.

'Hang on girl. I'll go when I'm ready. I want to ask Phillip about young Joe, if he'd heard any news. What a worrying turn of events, isn't it?'

The old woman looked straight at Phil, mock concern on her face. Phil replied.

'We haven't heard anything yet. We were out looking again this morning, but can't find any trace of him. I'm sure he's found somewhere to stay the night. He'll turn up soon.'

A wry smile crept onto Liz's face, as she spoke.

'I'm sure that's right Phil. He'll have no doubt found a bed for the night somewhere. We all know Joe isn't too fussy about where he beds down for the night.'

Mary had been holding her tongue, but had now heard enough of their poison.

'Well you'd know all about that, wouldn't you Liz?'

Kitty's face twisted and darkened, as she glared at Liz. Her granddaughter's cold cheeks reddened as she tried to avoid her nan's piercing eyes. Liz fumbled and stuttered, struggling to force out a response.

'How's your nan Mary?'

'She's fine.'

'Really? I'd heard she'd moved in with Beth.'

Mary scowled, but this time it was Phil's turn to seek to calm things.

The Storm

'It's been lovely speaking to you. We must get going. Enjoy the service.'

Phil tugged at Mary and the girl and began to move away from the old woman and her granddaughter. As they edged away Kitty muttered something under her breath. It wasn't loud enough to catch everything, but fragments of the words were caught by Phil and Mary.

'I hope this one fairs better than the last.'

Catching echoes of the cutting words, Mary jumped away from Phil and grabbed Kitty. Mary's eyes burned with rage, her grip crushing the old woman's arm.

'What did you say?'

Liz and Kitty looked startled, as the old woman fumbled with her words. For once the shock had taken the edge off her cruel wit.

'Nothing Mary. I didn't say anything. Now kindly let go of me.'

Liz reached for Mary's arm and tried to release her grip. As Liz leant towards Mary, she spat out her words.

'Let go of her now!'

Mary glared back at Liz, the menace in her eyes warning enough. Liz eased her hand back as Mary turned and continued to address Kitty.

'Now again I'll ask you and you're going to tell me if I keep you out here till I get it out of you. What did you say?'

'I...I...I just said. I hope everything works out for the best.'

'I know you and your kind Kitty Dawson. You have a wicked tongue. You've been spreading your bile in this village for too long. Now keep your thoughts to yourself. If I hear anyone, and I mean anyone speaking of this, I know where to come.'

Kitty snarled. Mary had thrown down the gauntlet, and Kitty loved nothing better than a fight. Mary's attempts to wound had only sharpened the old woman's steely edge.

'Before you start telling me what to do. You might want to get your own house in order first. I'm not the one spreading rumours about the town about your little creature. You need to be looking closer to home for that.'

Kitty paused as the two women glared at each other. Kitty continued with no let up in the bitterness in her voice.

'Remember this. Me and your nan have been around a lot of years. We've seen more things than you can ever imagine. This isn't the first time this kind of thing has happened. Watch your step, and keep a close eye on her. Don't say I didn't warn you. Now get out of my way.'

Kitty pushed past Mary, followed by Liz, as both of them stormed through the gates and up the pathway towards the church. Phil still clutched the girl, preventing her from falling. She looked weaker than ever, helpless, lost, and still shivering as the rain and wind lashed down at them.

'Leave them Mary. Ignore it. You know what they're like. Liz has never been the same since the accident, and we all know the likes of Kitty. There's another one peddling her superstitious rubbish. Come on.'

Mary looked back at Phil, her voice choked, close to tears.

'And Kitty's not the worst one, is she?'

Mary frowned. Phil knew who she meant. They had seen no sign of her this morning, but she would be here, somewhere. If not yet arrived, then waiting in the church.

'We can sort all that out later. Let's get inside.'

Phil stepped forward as Mary linked the girl from the other side. Mary paused, tugging them back.

'Are you sure this is a good idea Phil?'

'Yes. We're here now so let's get going.'

The three of them shuffled along the path tucked in behind more of the arriving congregation. Each small group huddled close to one another, trying to lessen the impact of the biting wind. The vicar gave half a smile as he saw Phil approach, which dissolved when he noticed the girl nestled between him and Mary. Struggling to conceal his discomfort, the vicar composed himself and reached out his hand to greet Phil.

'Good morning Phil, Mary. I trust you are well. I see you have brought your visitor. I've heard a lot about her. I must say I'm surprised to see you here. I thought the poor young thing would have wanted to rest after her ordeal.'

Phil took the vicar's hand with his powerful grip. He towered over the vicar who looked disheveled and windswept, white gown flapping, face dripping with rain. Phil held his grip, shaking hard as he spoke.

'Good morning Matthew. We're all well thank you, at least as well as can be expected. Yes, this is the girl. We're not sure of her name yet. You must forgive her, but she's still a bit fragile. I'm sure you heard about the circumstances in which I found her. We thought it was important the community got to meet her, that we showed her how warm and welcoming the people of the village are. We're all good Christian people, isn't that right Matthew?'

The vicar's weather beaten cheeks, seemed to deepen their crimson colour.

'Of course Phil. We are indeed all children of God. I'm sure we'll do whatever we can while she's with us. I trust her stay won't be long.'

'No. I'm hoping to take her to town once the weather let's up. Then we can get her home safe and sound.'

Father Matthew looked down at the girl. She was trembling even more, her eyes darting from side to side, the mumbling intensified. The girl's body swayed as she rocked back and forth on her feet. The vicar bent down and reached out his hand to her.

'Good morning child. Welcome to our community and the lord's house. All are welcome here. You're in good hands. Phil and Mary will take good care of you. I'm sure you'll find your way back to where you belong very soon.'

The vicar caught the eyes of Mary and Phil. It was an awkward look and Matthew stuttered as he struggled to move the conversation on.

'And what a dreadful turn of events with poor Joseph. Is there any news on his whereabouts?'

Phil shook his head.

'No, but I'm sure he'll turn up soon.'

'I've no doubt he will. We'll be sure to say a prayer for him this morning and I'll mention it in the sermon. Just in case anyone knows anything, but hasn't been able to share it yet, may I suggest they come to me in confidence if they have anything they'd like us to know? Not that I'm suggesting anything untoward has happened, of course. But you have to keep an open mind in these situations. People make enemies easily in such a small community. People know things, words get said, rumours spread, and before long no-one knows what is true anymore. Or who is a friend.'

Mary sensed Phil's simmering agitation again, and nudged him, ushering them all into the church. Mary exchanged a few final words with the vicar.

'Thank you Father. Your kindness and discretion are always appreciated. Please let us know if you do hear of anything.'

Phil, Mary and the girl filed through the door and into a small stone porch where a second arched oak door led into the main building. The church was freezing, with the high ceiling and stone walls doing little but crush whatever heat there may have been. At the rear of the church to the left was a stone font filled with holy water, and in the corner away from the door was a seating area. Three columns of pews stood alongside one another, lined row after row to the front where the lectern stood from which Father Matthew would give his sermon. Behind the lectern was the chancel and sanctuary. Here an altar stood under an ornate and colourful window in stained glass. Even on the darkest days the light would breathe life into each section of glass casting a dazzling glow across the people packed into the cold chancel.

The congregation sat pressed together, still wrapped in heavy overcoats and thick winter clothing. Most heads were lowered in silent reverence, or were weary from the heavy weekend and early start. A few sat back and stared into space, admiring the colours of the window with lips moving in quiet prayer. Then there were the fidgets, those with prying eyes, forever looking this way and that, searching for signs, the next gossip. They would come away with shreds of truth, fragments of fiction they could whip into a flurry of speculation and lies. Ella was one of those. Seated already, on the end, midway down the central column, her back straight, hands folded, a sullen scowl scanning the room. Phil spotted the old woman first, Mary seconds later. She wasn't in her usual place, the seats Phil, Mary and her most often took. Ella had switched allegiance and homes, and now sat among strangers.

Phil and Mary crept along the central aisle, sheltering the girl, tucked between other families, passing layer upon layer of rows. As they approached their usual space heads began to turn, and eyes fixed upon them. Even the reverent and pious looked up, or paused for a moment from their prayers to gaze at those they knew and the mysterious stranger. All were struck by her dark, tender beauty, how fragile and vulnerable she looked alongside the mite of Phil. Those of warmer hearts saw the fear, while the cold felt only suspicion. The girl was a mirror reflecting either the good or darkness that lay within themselves. Mary wrapped the trembling creature in her arms, held her as tight as she could, all the while whispering words of reassurance in the girl's ear, words she may not understand, but would sense in the caring voice. Phil caught the eye of some of those watching, and smothered the cynicism in their look with a menacing glare. As the three of them reached Ella, the old woman looked forward, never turning her head, not even to acknowledge their presence. Ella's wizened, sunken lips added greater depth to the misery of her scowl.

Phil led them to their usual row, squeezing past as others stood to let them through. They sat and

The Storm

waited, the girl cowering in between Phil and Mary. Silence echoed in the cavernous depths of the nave, the heat of a hundred eyes burning holes in the back of their heads. Mary snuggled into the girl, trying to conceal the severity of her shaking, smothering her fear. The suffocating tension closed in around them, as heavy and overpowering as the black clouds outside, a blanket of suspicion. The vicar tiptoed along the aisle, still ragged and windswept, his dark hair messy and wet. He entered a door at the rear of the chancel and returned with fresh, dry robes, hair combed across his head. Taking his place at the altar the service began.

Phil's mind meandered as the words of the service washed over him. Images of the young girl that had troubled him for much of the night kept returning. Flashing into his head, he struggled to cast them aside. There were visions of Joe, and Phil felt sick to the stomach with the possibilities. He wanted to believe the rational explanation, but sensed something was wrong. Phil had a good sense for these things, and enough experience to know. He listened to his sense even when it told him things he wanted to deny. Mary tended to the girl by their side. The trembling seemed to have eased as Mary comforted and nursed her like a baby, as if she was her own child. The veil of daydreams lifted as Phil caught some of the words of the vicar's sermon.

'And the parable tells us how:

On one occasion an expert in the law stood up to test Jesus. 'Teacher,' he asked, 'What must I do to inherit eternal life?'

'What is written in the Law?' He replied.

'How do you read it?' He answered.

'Love the Lord your God with all your heart and with all your soul and with all your strength and with all your mind'; and, 'Love your neighbour as yourself.'

'You have answered correctly,' Jesus replied. 'Do this and you will live.'

But he wanted to justify himself, so he asked Jesus, 'And who is my neighbour?'

In reply Jesus said: 'A man was going down from Jerusalem to Jericho, when he was attacked by robbers. They stripped him of his clothes, beat him and went away, leaving him half dead. A priest happened to be going down the same road, and when he saw the man, he passed by on the other side. So too, a Levite, when he came to the place and saw him, passed by on the other side. But a Samaritan, as he traveled, came where the man was; and when he saw him, he took pity on him. He went to him and bandaged his wounds, pouring on oil and wine. Then he put the man on his own donkey, brought him to an inn and took care of him. The next day the Samaritan took out two denarii and gave them to the innkeeper. 'Look after him,' he said, 'and when I return, I will reimburse you for any extra expense you may have.'

Which of these three do you think was a neighbour to the man who fell into the hands of robbers?'

The expert in the law replied, 'The one who had mercy on him.'

Jesus told him, 'Go and do likewise.'

There was a long pause as the words of the sermon echoed around the church. Phil twisted his body round and stared across at Ella. The old woman's head remained still, looking straight ahead, ignored him. As he panned round Phil caught the eye of Kitty who glared back at him and sneered.

The Storm

The vicar announced they were about to sing a hymn. Just then the doors burst open. One of the widows from the boats on the beach stumbled into the church. She was frantic, screaming, crying, and screeching in hysterics.

'He's gone. He's gone. My Tom. They've taken him.'

Phil jumped to his feet and pushed through the crowd gathering round her already. There were whispers, muttering, staring eyes, a number were looking back at Mary and the girl. Mary cradled the girl as she trembled and cowered. Her lips were moving, as she chanted under her breath. The vicar had followed Phil, and now nursed Tom's mother in his arms as she continued to scream.

'My boy. My boy. They've taken him.'

The vicar rocked her, trying to calm her.

'Who's taken him Ivy? Who's taken him?'

As the word 'taken' was repeated over and over, it seemed to echo around the church. More eyes turned to Mary and the girl. More sneers and suspicious looks. Mary could see them, feel them all, casting their judgement. Mary was not concerned though. She was too preoccupied with comforting the girl. Then Mary saw them, all three standing together - Dot, Kitty, and Ella. Their stares pierced through the crowd and stabbed at Mary. Ignoring them, she looked down at the girl, and pulled her in tight. Mary whispered.

'It's OK. We'll get you out of here. Don't worry it'll be alright.'

Phil had returned and took Mary's arm.

'Get her out of here. I'll see what's going on.'

Mary pushed through the crowd, her arm and shawl draped over the girl, protecting her from the accusative looks. Mary saw it in the eyes, could see their judgement. Some lips were moving, and Mary caught fragments of the bitter mumblings.

'Everything was fine till she arrived.'

'She doesn't belong here.'

'We all know what she is.'

'She has to go.'

Pushing their way to the doorway, Mary and the girl disappeared. As Phil watched them go he noticed three youngsters from the boats standing by the door. They were Tom's friends, Phil had seen them messing about on the beach and moor. One of the girls was always with him, and had been there when Tom asked Phil if he could work his boat. The commotion continued at the back of the church, as all eyes focused on Tom's mother now Mary and the girl had gone. Ivy was settling, but the crowd were becoming more uneasy, stoked by the mutterings of the mob. Phil pushed through them and made for the door. The youngsters saw Phil approaching and turned to leave. Phil shouted.

'Wait a moment. I need to speak to you.'

All three paused, closing the door and looking at each other as Phil stepped into the porch and pulled the inner door shut behind him. The small hallway was freezing, and the gusts of icy wind whistled as they slipped under the gaps in the outer door. The young friends stood in a line waiting for their elder. Phil looked them up and down in turn and spoke.

'I need to know what happened with Tom.'

There was silence, as each of them stared at the stone floor. Phil waited, focusing on Mable who looked up and caught his stare. Phil place a hand on her shoulder and spoke.

'It's Mable, isn't it?'

She nodded and Phil continued.

'You came to see me with Tom a few weeks ago, didn't you?'

There was another brief nod of recognition.

'If Tom's in danger I need to know. I'm not interested in what you've been up to. That stays between us. The important thing is finding Tom.'

Mable looked down at the floor again, then across at the others. Annie looked away but Jack nodded. Mable swallowed and sighed.

'We were in the abandoned house last night. We didn't mean any harm. It was Tom's idea. He said it'd be fine, that he'd been there before. We just wanted to see the place, how the rich folk live. I'm sorry.'

There was a pause as Mable fought back tears. Phil leant forward, smiled and shook his head.

'Don't worry. That's not important, I just need to know about Tom. How did he disappear?'

Mable wiped her eyes as she answered.

'I don't know. I didn't see anything. He was there when we fell asleep last night and gone this morning. The back door was open and he left a candlestick by the door. The thing is we didn't have a key to the door, so I can't see how he unlocked it. It must have been opened by someone with a key.'

The young girl began to weep, plunging her face into her hands. Phil crouched and put his arm around her, then turned to the other two.

'What about you? Did either of you see or hear anything?'

Jack replied as Annie shook her head.

'We were both sleeping. The first we knew of it was when Mable woke us and told us he'd gone.'

Phil nodded.

'I'm sure we'll find him. You say you were at the house?'

Jack replied.

'Yes. We slept in one of the sitting rooms. We didn't damage or take anything. We were just having a bit of fun.'

Phil stood up tall again.

'Come with me. Show me where you stayed.'

Phil opened the heavy outer door and led them into the churchyard leaving the jabbering of the mob behind. The congregation were stirring a new storm of speculation, accusation, and suspicion. Strange events were unfolding and they wanted answers, and where there were none they would create their own. This was how it started. Phil knew that. He had to find answers soon, before things spiralled beyond control. Without answers Phil knew how this might end.

10

Phil walked down the garden steps, as Mable and the others followed. They had been to the house, looked at the room in which they slept, searched the other rooms. They found no clues. All that remained were someone's memories gathering dust. The back door that had been left ajar, the stump of a candlestick stood alone on a small table by the door. There were broken footprints in the sand, by the entrance to the porch. Phil followed the trail, Tom's young friends close behind, walking heads bowed, in silence.

They exited the gate at the bottom of the garden and crossed the promenade to a set of steps leading to the beach. The trail of prints were more pronounced on the sand. There was a set of two, the first small and lighter in imprint, the second much larger suggesting someone heavier. Phil and the others followed them to the shoreline where the footsteps ended as they entered the sea. Looking out over the waves, Phil was lost in thought. Meanwhile Mable, Annie and Jack watched and waited. Mable spoke to fill the awkward silence.

'What is it?'

Phil pointed at the sand.

'These footprints lead from the house. They end here.'

'How do you know they're Tom's? There are lots of footprints.'

'I don't for sure, but these are different. They're barefoot. They start just outside the back door. Tom's shoes were still in the house. His clothes were by the fireplace in the room.'

Mable looked at the others and frowned. They exchanged stares as Phil's words began to sink in. Jack spoke.

'You think he came out here undressed and walked into the sea? It doesn't make any sense. Why would he do that?'

Phil moved towards them, resting his arm on Mable's shoulder. The young girl lowered her head and began to sob. Annie stared at her feet, kicking the sand, as Jack gazed out to sea, tears filling his eyes. Phil spoke.

'I really don't know what happened. There are more than one set of footprints, so it may not be Tom. Let's not jump to any conclusions just yet. Let me take you all home. I'll round up some people and we'll look for Tom. Don't worry I'm sure he'll turn up fine.'

Phil wrapped his arms around Mable and Annie and led the three friends along the windswept beach towards the village of boats huddled together at the far end. This was where their mothers waited, each in despair over the child they might have lost, weeping for the child of their friend and neighbour who was lost already.

....

Ella sat in her new throne, as Phil shook himself down and removed his coat. Passing it to Beth, she laid it on the back of a chair by the table, then went to tend to the children playing on the floor in the far corner. Phil took a chair opposite Ella. She ignored him, her face expressionless as she stared into the fire. Phil spoke, his voice calm, showing no hint of the swirling emotions inside.

'Ella, I need to talk to you about the past day or so. There's something going on.'

Phil paused then continued.

'You mentioned something the other day, something about seeing this before. Do you know anything you're not telling me?'

The old woman shuffled in the chair and grunted, still looking into the fire as she replied.

'You need to get rid of the girl. She needs to go back where she belongs and soon, otherwise there'll be more of this, more men will be taken.'

Phil leant forward, moving closer to the chair, trying to catch Ella's eye, hoping she would look at him. Instead Ella kept facing forward. Phil replied.

'What do you mean, back where she belongs? I will get her home, but I can't do that till I can reach the town. As soon as the storm lifts we'll go. What more can I do?'

Ella laughed, a low muffled laugh mocking Phil's words.

'You don't understand, do you? They won't be able to find her home. There's only one place she belongs and I know where it is already.'

Phil frowned, as he gazed at Ella's cracked face, still showing no change in expression. Phil waited for Ella to continue. When it was clear she would not, Phil replied.

'Where?'

Ella turned her head and looked him in the eye. Without expression or emotion she answered.

'Her home is the sea.'

The old woman looked away, back into the comforting warmth of the flames.

Phil slumped back in the chair, pondered what Ella had said, as well as all she had left unsaid. He spoke.

'You're not making a lot of sense Ella. How can she be from the sea?'

Ella remained silent, impassive, continued playing with her lips as she often did. The old woman stretched, then sucked them, drawing them into the toothless chasm of her mouth. It was clear Ella had said all that she wanted to. The playful giggles of Beth and the children drifted from the corner of the room. Phil looked across, staring at the faces of the children. He jumped to his feet and reached for his coat.

'Thanks Beth. I'm done here for now.'

Beth climbed to her feet and came to the door just as Phil was about to leave. She whispered.

'I couldn't help but overhear. I know she's not making a lot of sense. If you want more you might want to speak to Kitty or Dot. You know what the three of them are like, a coven of old witches, but they'll know. I saw them all chatting at the back of the church earlier. Kitty might be best. She can't help telling you that she knows. You'll get more out of her than anyone.'

Beth winked and smiled, as Phil leant over and pecked her on the cheek.

'Thanks Beth. Take care.'

As the door swung open Phil braced himself as he was struck by driving wind and rain again. Beth watched him bound down the street, as she eased the door shut, and returned to the children playing. The two innocent young girls lay on a carpet with their rag dolls singing rhymes. Susan chanting the same verse over and over:

'Dark girl, lonely girl
Where is't that you do come?
Beware the sons of fishermen
For the sea is where I'm from

The Storm

Dark girl, lonely girl
Why is't that you do cry?
I am longing for family
In dark water they do lie'

....

'Is Kitty here? I need to speak to her.'

Liz peered through the crack in the door, and Phil heard a voice from inside.

'Let him in.'

Liz opened the door and ushered Phil inside. The room was almost a copy of the other houses in the street. Snug and comfortable, there was a random assortment of furniture surrounding the fireplace that dominated the space. Kitty sat knitting at the kitchen table, dressed in her usual dour clothing, a cup of something medicinal placed on the table in front of her.

'Let me get your coat.'

Liz helped Phil remove his jacket and pulled out a chair at the table. She gestured for him to take a seat.

'Would you like a cup of tea?'

'No thanks. I won't be staying long. I just wanted to ask your nan a couple of things.'

Kitty continued with her knitting, pretending to concentrate on the needles despite being able to do this in her sleep. There was the gentle click of the metal as the old woman tugged and teased the wool. Phil looked on, waiting for her to speak, but it was clear he would have to break the silence.

'I've just been to see Ella. I wanted to put an end to these rumours you're all spreading about the girl.

She told me a little about what's been said, but it makes no sense.'

Kitty waited a while then spoke, continuing to rattle the needles and flick the wool.

'So what did she say?'

'Just that the girl doesn't belong here, we need to get her back home as quickly as we can, and that her home is the sea.'

Kitty stopped and looked up, her stern expression darkened even more.

'That's what she told you, is it? Well there's no more I can tell you.'

Phil shook his head, as Liz watched on, perched just over the shoulder of Kitty. Phil replied.

'I don't get it. What does she mean her home is the sea? I found her on the beach. She was saved from the sea. She was in the shipwreck. She would have died if I hadn't found her. I can't put her back, can I?'

Kitty stopped knitting, and placed the needles and wool on the table. Her eyes narrowed as she edged forward across the table.

'You don't understand Phillip. You didn't save her from the sea. You stole her from them and they want her back.'

A heavy veil of silence enveloped the room as the atmosphere thickened. Phil stared at Kitty then Liz. Both women looked grave, each with a knowing look, a blinding belief all they knew was true. It was a look of pity, for Phil, his naivety, and ignorance. He stumbled for words, such was the churn of thoughts tumbling in his head.

'Stole her? From who? I don't understand. Who wants her back?'

Liz pressed her hands down onto the shoulders of the old woman who lifted the needles and wool from

The Storm

the table and began to knit again. The brisk clicking began again, like a drummer driving out a beat in a steady, repetitive motion. Without looking up Kitty spoke.

'I've said all I will Phillip. It doesn't pay to speak their name. Misfortune comes to those who do.'

Liz moved towards the chair, took Phil's coat and handed it to him. She was silent, as she held out her arm. Phil knew it was over and he was no longer welcome. As he moved to the door, and was about to open it Kitty spoke again. The final word, as always.

'Be careful Phillip. Get rid of her or they'll take everything you love, and I mean everything. Ella is only saying this for your own good. It's you and Mary she's thinking of. You've suffered enough, be sure to heed our words.'

Liz gripped the door and ushered Phil out, slamming the door behind. Standing outside, battered by the storm again, he was oblivious to the brutal, relentless force. Phil had grown weary of the storm now, no longer cared, there were more worrying concerns. He needed to think straight, and plan the next move. Two people were missing and all the villagers saw was a mysterious girl. The events all happened under the veil of the storm. Was it a coincidence? Phil wasn't just battling against the storm, he also fought the growing wall of suspicion the community was building. They were proud people steeped in tradition. The past was an anchor in the midst of an uncertain future. They were good people, loyal and loving, but they feared the unexplained and unknown. The villagers would do anything to protect their own, and the wall was that protection. Time was running out. Phil set off for home, to Mary and the girl.

11

The girl lay sleeping while Mary and Phil sat at the table. Phil scraped the remaining gravy from his plate with a chunk of bread, devoured it, and licked his fingers. He played with his fork, twirling it between his fingers, while Mary sipped a glass of water. The silence between them was choking Mary, eventually she could stand it no longer.

'We need to talk.'

Phil peered across the table, the fork fell clattering against the plate.

'What about?'

Mary pushed her finger against her lips.

'Ssshhhh! you'll wake the girl!'

Phil looked puzzled, waiting for Mary to continue. As a veil of silence swept over them his mind wandered. After a moment he spoke.

'It's strange, isn't it? It's like having a child in the house again.'

Mary stood and shuffled round the table. Picking up his plate, she moved to the sink, turning and staring back at her husband. Mary's face was ashen white. Phil sat up, waiting for her to speak. Mary spoke, her voice almost a whisper.

'I've something important to tell you.'

Phil could feel his heart racing. Mary's breath quivered as she let out a sigh. Phil could wait no longer for her to continue.

'What is it?'

There was another long silence, with only the pounding rhythm of their hearts. Then Mary uttered the last words Phil had expected. Words he had longed to hear. Words that he craved, but feared as well.

'I'm with child again.'

A bolt shot through Phil, as the words struck him, echoing in his head. They hung there, waiting for him to clutch at each one. Mary's body stiffened, as she waited for his reaction. Phil stared at the table, shaking his head. When he spoke his voice was shaking.

'I don't know what to say.'

Mary looked on, small beads of sweat trickling down her brow.

'This is good news Phil, isn't it?'

Mary's voice was cracking, every ounce of her emotion within her question. Time seemed to stand still as she waited for Phil to respond. He jumped to his feet, moved to Mary and wrapped his arms around her, hugging her tight. Her anxiety eased, as she melted into his arms, head lain against his chest as Phil rocked them back and forth. After a while Mary whispered.

'I wasn't sure how you would feel about it.'

Phil stroked his wife's hair, staring at the wall, lost in his thoughts. Mary spoke again.

'It'll be a fresh start for us, help us get over the accident.'

Phil stiffened, stopped rocking, and loosened his grip. He turned and moved to the table. Mary spoke, her voice now agitated.

'I'm sorry, I shouldn't have brought it up.'

Standing hunched over the table, Phil rubbed his eyes and shook his head.

'I'm still finding it hard to deal with what happened.'

Filling a mug with water, Phil took a long drink banging the mug down.

'I'm happy about the baby. Of course, I am. But the other stuff will take time. This brings it back that's all.'

Mary edged closer to her husband, pausing within arms reach.

'We have to move on. Maybe now it's time to forget.'

Phil glared at Mary, his face fizzing with anger, a look she seldom saw. His voice trembled with emotion, on the verge of breaking.

'How do you expect me to forget?'

Phil paused, their eyes locked together. Mary wanted to reach out and comfort him, but something prevented her. Phil's eyes were pleading with her, his voice a cracked whisper.

'You've never forgiven me, have you?'

Tears began to emerge from the corner of Mary's eyes, one by one until soon they were streaming down her face. The couple stood together, alone, pondering their past and wondering what the future may hold. As his wife lowered her head, and sobbed into her hands Phil gazed at the veil in the corner of the room. His thoughts drifted to the girl sleeping on the other side. Anxiety sliced through him, fear, uncertainty and doubt. He was reminded of what might lie ahead, for the girl, Mary and his unborn child.

....

The sea was tranquil, and the summer sunlight shimmered off the clear crystal blue waters. Phil sat at the brow of the small boat, leaning against the side, puffing on his pipe, letting the smoke drift up his nostrils as he inhaled. His eyes felt heavy, as the mid-afternoon heat hypnotised him. The air was clear, but thick with the suffocating heat. A young girl sat playing at the other end of the boat, chatting away with her rag dolls, acting out a game, as children do. Long black hair flowed down her back, and bright red lips were set within soft delicate skin. She was an angel, their angel, the gift for which Phil and Mary had prayed so long.

Phil watched as his daughter sat lost in her own world, oblivious to the miles of sea around, stretching out like a continuous sheet of glass. The boat bobbed, the gentlest of movements, enough to rock Phil to sleep, as a baby in the arms of a doting mother. He drifted away, as his mind surrendered to the charms of sun and sea. As he slept Phil could still hear quiet chatter seeping into his dreams, then laughter. Phil dreamt of a fairground, the annual summer fayre, when the beach and promenade were packed with deck chairs. People flocked from miles around to soak up the sunshine, paddle in the refreshing waters, and rest on the soft, soothing sands. The wealthy would come to admire the beauty of the bay, a sight the poorest saw every day. Sometimes the villagers forgot how lucky they were, but a day never went by when Phil wasn't thankful.

The playful laughter of children in the dream mingled with the giggling in the background. A kaleidoscope of bright colours swamped Phil, candy floss pink, sunshine yellows, and ocean blues. All the while shafts of sunlight warmed his face. He felt at peace, wrapped in a perfect moment. Then something changed. There was a scream and Phil saw a woman running along the sands towards him. She was some way off in the distance, but he could see her waving, the scream getting louder all the time. Phil knew who it was, he would recognise her anywhere. It was Mary. Phil started to run towards his wife, trying to decipher the words wrestling within the shrill cry of the scream. He snatched at them, catching only fragments at first - Phil, help, save her, Phil, look out, save her.

Phil stopped running and spun round. There was clear water and dazzling light, and the laughter of people paddling. Then he saw them, a sea of bodies swarming across the sand. Panic built as he looked everywhere for his daughter. Staring back at Mary, he was willing her to reach him, but she didn't seem to be any nearer. His wife was running, screaming, and he could still hear her words, but she was trapped in the distance, as though running on the spot. Phil swirled full circle, the dizziness of the movement mixing with the panic and confusion in his head.

Something triggered in Phil's head, and he realised this was all a dream. The beach began to dissolve, and the sea disappear as his eyes opened and caught the piercing sunlight. He rubbed them, and sat up. The silence struck him. Phil looked round the boat. She was gone. Jumping to his feet, Phil scrambled to the back of the boat, looking under a piece of tarpaulin, then over the side. The calm, clear water glistened, but there was no movement. Sickness ran through Phil as the full force of terror and desperation overwhelmed him. His eyes darted this way and that, looking for anything beneath the water, any sign. Then he noticed it. Floating a few feet away from the boat was a rag doll. It swirled and swayed in the water, as though sliding on ice.

Phil scrambled to undress, throwing off his clothes and shoes, and diving into the sea. The cold stole his

The Storm

breath as he entered the water, flapping about, dipping his head under then resurfacing again. Phil was a poor swimmer. Despite being a fisherman his lumbering body was not meant for the water. The frantic efforts to find the girl mixed with fear of the water began to take over. Phil was struggling to breathe, and was close to drowning. Still he would not give up, could not give up. Again and again he plunged under the water, the sea enveloping him, as though entering another world. The silence of the surface was replaced with a strange serenity. Phil searched, but struggled to see far, as the salt water stung his eyes. Soon the air in his lungs burst free and he spluttered and coughed as he rose into the air again, gasping, clinging to life.

The boat drifted away from Phil, and he paddled to reach it, gripping onto the side, it lurched as it took the weight of his body. Clinging on with one arm, and paddling with the other, Phil swept under the surface, feeling for any sign of his daughter. He wept, screaming occasional words, calling out her name - Ellie. Phil knew if he let go of the boat it would be the end. The best chance was to cling to the side and keep looking, hoping she would surface, somewhere. All he could see was a smooth, shimmering crystal sheet of glass stretching for miles in all directions. The truth began to hit him, the realisation that it was over, that his Ellie was lost.

Phil pulled himself into the boat, just managing to drag himself inside. He lay face down, head pressed against the damp wooden boards, sobbing. The tears ran into the saliva that clung to his trembling lips. He muttered to himself, fighting through his crying.

'No! Please. No!'

Over and over again he repeated the words, all the while weeping, a burning in his chest as his heart crumbled. Minutes drifted into hours, as the boat swayed in the eery silence. Then Phil felt something, someone shaking him. He rolled over and looked up into the dazzling sunlight. There was a silhouette, as someone stood over him. Their hand reached down and pressed against his shoulder, prodding him. Then the piercing light began to fade and die, and everything dissolved into darkness. The gentle swaying of the boat ceased and the heat of the summer's day was replaced by a cooler biting air. Phil heard a voice.

'Phil. It's me Phil. Wake up.'

Phil sat up and there was Mary. He lay dripping in cold sweat, throat dry, lips stitched together. Prising them free, ripping off layers of tender skin, Phil coughed out a few words.

'I'm fine. I was just having a terrible dream.'

Mary stroked the hair on her husband's forehead, moving it aside, and brushing beads of sweat from his brow.

'Was it the same one?'

Phil paused, unsure of his answer.

'I think so. It's been a while.'

Mary leant down and hugged Phil, her touch warm and tender as she stroked his hair. Phil fought back tears, as the haze lifted and the bitterness of reality crept in. Neither of them noticed the girl standing behind, watching them. She was just beyond the veil, peering at the couple, as the light of the fire flickered in the dark pools of her eyes. The girl looked calm, serene, but with a look of sorrow on her face, as a single tear trickled down her cheek. The girl let the veil surrounding the bed fall as she returned to the bed. Lying like a foetus, her eyes open, tears streaming, as lips moved, muttering in silence.

....

The room was dark and quiet, but for the occasional crackle of the dying embers, and gentle rattle of a snore. A girl stood at the base of the bed and looked on as Kitty slept. The white sheet and knitted patchwork blanket covered all but the old woman's wizened face. Mouth wide open, Kitty's thick, grey hair was wrapped in a bundle and covered by a night cap. All the while the girl stood and waited, arms by her side, hair flowing across her chest, and down her dark gown. Moving round to the side of the bed, the girl sat by Kitty's side, hovering, studying her as she lay helpless, frail and vulnerable. The girl lowered her head towards the old woman's face, gliding over her, sniffing her skin, studying every crack and wrinkle. Easing back, she paused, their mouths were parallel, her dark eyes burning through the eyelids of the old woman.

Kitty began to stir, sensing something was there, feeling the stale breath upon her. Opening her eyes she saw the girl pressing down upon her. She tried to scream, but as her mouth opened so did the girl's. Kitty felt the air being sucked from her lungs, every piece being drawn from deep within. The old woman fought for air, desperate to breathe, but the girl was too strong. Eyes wide with terror, the girl remained locked upon her, continuing to drain her victim of life. Kitty began to struggle, but the sheet was tucked tight, and her arms were trapped. She tried to move her head, frantic, forcing a scream, but no sound would break from her burning throat. Paralysed, locked in an airless vacuum, her eyes began to bulge, small cracks of bloodshot creeping across them. The veins in the old woman's temple were turning blue, her face gathering a deep shade of scarlet. Only the last fragments of life were left. The girl's eyes lit up just as Kitty's went blank.

Silence enveloped the room. The girl stared at the lifeless face locked in terror. Easing her head back, the girl gazed down at the old woman, her vacant eyes wide open, along with the chasm of her toothless mouth. The girl rose to her feet and glided to the bottom of the bed. Pausing, she stood over Kitty, her eyes shifting up and down the corpse a few times. She lifted her gaze onto the wall above the bed. Standing motionless, waiting, the girl smiled. Her work was done.

DAY THREE

Chris Ord

12

'Have you heard about poor Kitty?'

Father Matthew's voice echoed through the church.

'I have. I can't believe it.'

Phil sat at the front pew, Father Matthew alongside, the condensation from their breath forming puffs of icy clouds as it hit the air. The vicar wore his usual white gown and collar, but was draped in a thick overcoat. Beads of rainwater still clung to him, his face flushed red, fresh from the ravages of the storm outside. The storm still showed no sign of letting up, and continued its assault on the village. Phil was hunched forward leaning on his knees.

'So why've you asked me here? Was it to tell me about Kitty?'

The vicar turned to face Phil, leaning his arm against the back of the pew.

'It's partly that, but there are other things we need to talk about.'

The vicar cleared his throat.

'What do you make of these strange happenings in the past few days?'

Phil stroked his beard.

'I don't know.'

Matthew shuffled again, trying to tease some comfort from the hard wooden surface.

'First the shipwreck, then the disappearance of Joe and young Tom. Now this.'

Phil sat up and stared at the vicar.

'I'm sorry about Kitty, but she was in her eighties. I'm sure there's nothing more to it than that. Let's not read something into everything.'

'That's not how Liz sees it. She seems to think there's more to it.'

Phil snapped.

'She's lost her nan. Of course, she's upset. I doubt she's thinking straight. But we need to stop this dangerous gossip. It's getting out of hand and won't do any of us any good.'

Father Matthew waited, allowing Phil time to settle, cautious not to agitate him further.

'How is Mary?'

'Fine.'

'And the girl?'

Phil glared at Matthew.

'She's pretty much the same. The sooner I can get her to town and clear everything up the better. She's terrified. She needs to be home with her family. They'll be able to look after her better at the hospital in town until we can find them and get her home.'

There was a long pause. Matthew reached down, picked up a hymn book, and began flicking through it.

'Do you have a favourite hymn Phil?'

Phil thought before replying.

'To Be A Pilgrim.'

'Ah yes. It's a beautiful hymn. With such an important message. It's very fitting for a man like you Phil. You're a man of courage, honour, someone of great principle. People admire you, love you for it. This community needs people like you Phil. Maybe we need to remind you of that more often.'

Phil looked puzzled, a half smile on his face, trying to conceal his discomfort. He cleared his throat.

'Thank you, but there's no need.'

The vicar continued to thumb through the pages of the hymn book as he replied.

'Men like you always see the good in people. It's a wonderful quality, and not something you should ever lose, Phil.'

'I guess not.'

'It's different for a man in my position. Sadly, I often see the other side. In fact, I deal with it every day. The darkness. The evil. There's a lot of it in this world. They're two sides of the same coin. You can't have one without the other. You might even say we need the darkness. It makes the light seem brighter.'

Phil continued to play with his beard, watching as Matthew played with the book. All the while the vicar looked down, pausing at random pages, scanning the words and moving on. The vicar seemed to be seeking reassurance from either the action or the words. Still gazing at the pages, Father Matthew continued.

'There's darkness in our community. Some is just good people in bad circumstances making the wrong decisions. Every now and then I'm confronted with something worse, something evil. I don't always recognise it at first. It often comes disguised. The devil is always looking to deceive.'

He paused a moment.

'Eventually I recognise it. I suppose I have to. I've come to know it in many shapes and forms. Sometimes the most surprising, the innocent and the beautiful. It's my job to drive it out, for the good of us all. My duty is to God and this community.'

Matthew stopped fumbling with the book and looked at Phil who coughed as he spoke.

'I'm not sure what you're getting at?'

The vicar stared at Phil, his face stern.

'Good men struggle to see evil. Their goodness blinds them. Think about the last few days Phil, look closely at all that has happened and all that you love.'

The vicar returned the hymn book, stood, and placed his arm on Phil's shoulder.

'Think about what I've said Phil. That's all I ask.'

Father Matthew shuffled towards the chancel and entered the door at the side. Phil watched as the vicar disappeared, then gazed up at the stained glass windows above the altar. The light outside was dull and cast a lifeless glow through the so often vibrant colours. Phil had sat in these seats a hundred times or more. It was a second home since childhood, a place of solace and comfort. In all those times he had never studied the beauty of the small fragments of multi-coloured glass. Each piece entwined to form a picture of such beauty, one transformed by the myriad shades of light, coming alive and dying depending on the moods of the weather, or time of day and year. Five narrow columns reached to the sky, in the centre was the image of Jesus, draped in a red cloak, arms raised in blessing, ascending to meet his Father. Either side of him were two winged angels, and above them an assortment of mythical animals: a Griffin; a Unicorn; and a Phoenix. Vivid blues and greens, reds and yellows, all shapes and sizes, each different, each unique, combining to make something of great beauty. Alone the fragments of glass were nothing, but together they formed something bold and magnificent.

Phil sat awhile and pondered Father Matthew's words. His thoughts turned to the night before, and the dream, the one he had dreamt so many times before. It had been a while, and certainly some time since it was as vivid. The images hung over him darker than the clouds still stretching across the stormy skies. A dull ache pressed in the back of his mind, pushing on all his thoughts, sucking the joy from every moment. This was how he had been since the accident, the ache and dark shadows would never leave his mind.

Phil stood and made his way towards the doorway. As he approached the heavy oak door he heard Matthew's voice from behind. Phil turned and saw him standing by the altar.

'Think about what I've said Phil. Nothing is more important than those you love.'

....

A piercing pain shot through Mary's stomach, pausing as she washed the plate, gasping for breath. It came again, this time harder. Buckled over Mary struggled to a chair by the table. Leaning forward Mary clutched her stomach and inhaled, long, deep breaths. There was a presence, something at her left shoulder. Mary looked round to see the girl was standing there. She wore the same clothes Mary had given her on the first day, worn them day and night, even slept in them. Mary was struck once more by the girl's beauty, despite the fear still etched in every expression. The tears had gone for now, and the panic attacks had eased. Mary noticed the girl was trembling.

They gazed at one another, each transfixed, eyes locked together, deep in thought. Then Mary noticed something she had not seen before, the faintest of smiles crept onto the girls lips. It was warm and gentle, lighting her face, bathing her beauty in a subtle charm. The jabbing pain came again. Mary winced and pulled her arms in tight, hugging her stomach, letting out a cry. The girl fell to her knees, the smile gone, replaced with a grim look of concern. Easing Mary's body back, the girl beckoned her to stand, helping Mary to her feet. Mary's legs were weak and the numbness left by the pain was crippling her. Tears trickled from the corners of her eyes.

The girl knelt in front of Mary and laid her cheek against her stomach. Mary felt a soothing warmth running through her lower body. Then she heard a sound. At first it was a quiet humming sound, but it picked up in volume until the girl was singing a soft, enchanting melody. It was a lullaby, without words, just a lyrical undulating sway of melody and sounds. The notes danced back and forth like waves on the sea.

Mary felt her eyes closing, drifting off into a half-sleep. Still conscious of the song and surroundings, but being drawn into the dreamy chambers of her mind. Images floated through her head, Phil, her mother and father, the unborn child, and Ellie, the daughter they had lost. It was Ellie's face Mary saw most of all. Her long, dark hair, and pretty, delicate face. The cherry lips that were always locked in the warmest smile. Ellie was reaching out to Mary. It was so real she could almost feel her daughter's touch again. Then Ellie's face changed, locked in a look of panic and alarm. Her outstretched hand couldn't reach Mary, their fingertips almost touched, but now were drifting further apart. Ellie's panic turned to terror and pleading as she was swept away, and faded into the distance.

Mary felt tears running down her cheek, and a bitter taste in her mouth. The girl was still on her knees before her, head on Mary's stomach, singing the

The Storm

lullaby. The pain had gone, the numbness eased, the singing stopped and the girl got to her feet. They faced each other, and the warm smile returned as the girl gazed at Mary. They were silent, watching for what seemed like an age, then the girl placed her hand against Mary, stroking the skin around her naval. She looked into Mary's eyes, still giving Mary a comforting look of warmth and reassurance. Then her lips parted and began to form a word. At first it was just the faintest whisper, so soft Mary couldn't be sure. Then her lips pressed together, parted and the word came again, though this time louder. Mary heard it now, a single word, the first the girl had spoken since her arrival. The word was cloaked in a strange and heavy accent, but it was English.

'Baby.'

Mary waited, just to be sure she wasn't dreaming. The girl whispered it again.

'Baby.'

Mary nodded and smiled.

'Yes, baby. I'm going to have a baby.'

The girl's face opened up into a huge and inviting smile, as though she was about to burst into laughter. She stopped whispering the word, looked at Mary with a delirious delight. Mary's face was half puzzled, half pleasure. She too wanted to laugh, but then the girl placed her fingertips against each of Mary's temples and closed her eyes. The girl's face was sterner now, locked in concentration. Mary studied the gentle curve of her cheekbones, mesmerised and bemused by the behaviour, looking for signs, any hint of a reaction. Mary's wonder soon turned to worry as the girl's face grew darker, and more grim. The girl became agitated, breathing harder, and shaking. Her eyes opened wide as she removed her hands and fell back against the table. Mary jumped forward trying to catch the girl as she fell.

'What is it? What did you see?'

Fear gripped the girl as she cowered away, sliding on the floor. Mary edged forward, reaching down for the girl's arm, but she snapped it away and shuffled away to the corner of the room. Mary eased towards her, beckoning all the while, the worried look now mixed with wounded confusion.

'What's wrong?'

The girl was shaking again, as another panic attack returned. She began to whimper, tears streaming from her eyes, a look of terror etched on her face. The brief glimmer of a young woman had been replaced by a child. Mary crept towards her, arms outstretched, whispering and reassuring the girl.

'It's OK.'

Mary crouched down wrapping her arms around her, pulling her body in tight as they both crumpled to the floor. Mary pressed the girl's head into her chest, rocking her to sleep, whispering words of comfort all the while.

'It's OK. There, there. It's over now.'

13

Mary sat alone in the church hall, her only company the wind as it whistled through gaps in the slates on the roof. She listened as the tiles rattled and the windows creaked. The room looked much larger than usual, empty but for the benches stacked away at the sides. The wooden flooring gave a hollow echo to any sound or movement. A few lanterns she had lit gave the only light, with most of the room cast in shadow. Mary waited, growing more impatient and agitated. As the minutes ticked by, she began to sense she was being watched. Tensions turned to fear, and after what seemed like an age the latch on the door clicked and from the shadows Ella appeared. Crooked, back arched over, waddling as she made her way towards her granddaughter.

'Thanks for coming Mary.'

'What is it nan? I haven't got long. Phil will be wondering where I've got to.'

'I best make it quick then.'

Ella's face was devoid of expression, reaching for a seat as Mary spoke.

'I'm sorry to hear about Kitty.'

Ella sat opposite Mary, lowered her head and replied. Her voice was quiet, with the familiar throaty growl.

'Yes. We all go back a long way. We grew up together, played in the back streets round here, hauled the lines together. She was a good woman despite what some might think of her. She thought everything of this community.'

Mary stood and put her arms round Ella, as the old woman continued.

'Kitty was loyal even if people didn't see it, but she was too loose with her tongue at times. I'm sure that's what did for her in the end.'

Mary moved round and retuned to her seat, looking puzzled she spoke.

'What do you mean?'

Ella paused before replying.

'We need to be careful. We're all in danger. They've come here for a reason and anyone who tries to stop them will be sorry.'

'I don't understand. You're not suggesting Kitty was murdered.'

Ella interrupted.

'I saw her body Mary, her face. Dot and me went to see her. We've seen that look before. We need to stick together. That's why I asked you here. I wanted to speak to you about the girl. We need to get her away from the house. You're not safe with her there. Phil doesn't see it. He's too good to see the poison in others. Except in me, of course.'

Ella cast a knowing stare at her granddaughter and continued.

'I know you're loyal to him Mary. I know how much you love him, but that's why I need you to listen. I'm saying this because I love both of you, and I don't want to see you come to any more harm.'

Mary paused, reeling from her nan's speculation on Kitty's death, trying to make sense of what the old woman was saying. Ella continued.

'Have you noticed anything strange about her?'

There was something not right about the girl. Mary sensed it, even though she didn't want to admit it. Mary composed herself, took a deep breath and spoke.

The Storm

'There are things which bother me. The girl's strange, but she's been through a lot, she must be terrified. We need to give her a chance. She'll be gone any day now. If only this storm would lift.'

Ella sighed.

'I know that, but we haven't got time. The storm is going nowhere until they get what they want. There's something more with this girl. I know you can see it, even if you don't want to for the sake of Phil.'

Ella stared at Mary waiting for a response. Her granddaughter sat silent, gazing at the floor, listening to the wind rattling through the roof tiles. Ella spoke.

'Do you not think it's too much of a coincidence, her being here when all this is going on.'

Ella got to her feet and stepped away. Mary sensed her discomfort.

'What is it nan?'

'Phil will never make up for what happened. No matter how many others he saves. That's what this is all about. He sees what you lost in the girl.'

A flurry of emotion flared up in Mary. She knew her nan was right, had known all along, but had chosen to ignore it.

'I know.'

Ella glared at Mary and spat out her words.

'She doesn't belong here Mary. She has to go. If she stays there'll be trouble. We need to get her out of that house.'

Ella waited for a reply, as the hush in the old hall huddled in around them, the only sound the cry of the wind and rattle of the rain. Mary looked up, her face forlorn, racked with confusion and guilt. Being here was an act of betrayal. She had to leave. As Mary was about to stand Ella clutched her granddaughter's head and pressed it into her chest. Lowering her head, Ella whispered.

'She might appear innocent, but I know their kind. She's here for a reason, or Phil wouldn't have found her. Either way, we have to get rid of her. They'll want her back.'

Mary was shocked, lifting her head and staring in horror at her nan. Ella shook her head, as Mary spoke.

'I don't want any harm to come to her. Maybe we could just find somewhere else for her to stay. Till the storm stops.'

Ella interrupted.

'I won't hurt her Mary. That would be the worst thing we could do. We don't want to anger them or they'll take revenge. We just need to get her back to where she belongs as soon as we can. If we don't return her they'll come.'

'Can we not wait till the storm ends.'

'Aren't you listening girl? The storm won't end as long as she's here. They bring the storm with them. It's here to trap us, keep us herded in like sheep. That's what they want, so we can't escape. They won't leave until they've got what they're after.'

There was a long pause as Ella stared at her granddaughter, waiting for a response. Mary wrestled with emotion, her mind swamped with conflicting images of Phil and the girl. Mary spoke, her voice brittle and cracked.

'Is there somewhere she can go? Somewhere safe?'

Ella sighed, hearing the pleading in Mary's voice, seeing the desperation.

'We can try and move her somewhere else, but what if she is one of them? We're just shifting the danger to someone else. Do you want to take that chance? Would you rather get rid of her or risk harming one of your own?'

Mary looked defeated. Lowering her head, she whispered her reply.

'So what do you want to do?'

Ella stepped back, shuffling her feet on the wooden floorboards. Most often stubborn and direct, the old woman seldom faced such discomfort, but this was Mary. She was all Ella had left in the world. Age had toughened the skin and hardened the heart, but Mary could still melt it like no-one else. As much as the words may hurt Mary, Ella was sure this was for the best. She was only doing this to protect her, and Phil, her family, their friends. That was all that mattered to Ella, the people she loved, even if they didn't see that. Ella swallowed, composed herself and spoke.

'She has to go Mary. We can't risk any more being taken. But we need to be careful. If they've sent her they won't like it if she returns without what she came for. Our best hope is that she's been washed up by accident, and they just want her back.'

Mary was confused, awash with this barrage of suspicion.

'Who are they? Who sent her? I don't understand. She was shipwrecked on a boat. No-one sent her here. Phil saved her life. You're not making any sense.'

Ella shook her head, before replying. Her voice was measured and calm. Years of hardship had brought bitterness, but also wisdom.

'Mary my dear, Phil and you are both so important to me. You're good people, the best I've known, and I've lived a long life and known a good few. But you're young and blinded by innocence at times. You don't see the girl for what she really is. That's part of their power. They can charm and seduce, especially men. You know what men are like. They're weak, especially when it comes to matters of the flesh. These creatures play on it. Neither of you understand what you're dealing with here.'

Ella paused, as the wind whistled louder than ever through the rafters.

'There's no use waiting for the storm to lift. It's here for a reason, because of her and her kind. It came to protect them and trap us. The storm is theirs, it'll only go when she goes. I've no doubt she was sent by them, and I know why they come.'

Mary was torn, her emotions becoming overwhelmed with frustration and anger. Ella could see Mary's torment. The old woman spoke in a softer voice. Despite being alone, it was as though Ella didn't want anyone else to hear, as if someone may be listening. There was a long pause as Ella considered her words.

'They come for the children, the unborn.'

Mary glared at Ella, searching her nan's expression, unable to disguise the horror in her face. Why had her nan mentioned that? Did she know? Only Phil and her knew of the baby, and Phil wouldn't betray the secret. Mary waited, thought hard about her next few words. Ella sensed there was something wrong. She could read her granddaughter as well as anyone, and knew when she was hiding something.

'What is it Mary? Is something wrong?'

Mary was on the verge of spitting it out, but something in the back of her mind dragged the words back.

'Nothing. It's not important. It can wait. So what do you want me to do?'

The Storm

They exchanged uncomfortable looks, as Ella replied.

'I'm not sure yet. We need to be careful. I've probably said too much as it is.'

The old woman paused and looked around the room. It was dark and silent but for the sounds of the storm. Ella was cautious though, afraid they were being watched. You could take no risks with them. She knew that. Ella moved closer to Mary.

'They've come for something, and they won't leave us be until they get it.'

Mary stared at her nan, a warning in her eye.

'And you promise you won't hurt her.'

Ella put her hand against Mary's cheek and smiled.

'I only want to get her back to where she belongs. The last thing I want to do is harm her or her kind. Our home is the sea too. We all have to live together.'

This had to end, and Ella feared the outcome. The old woman knew she had to take control and put a stop to this. Realising the time, Mary jumped to her feet.

'I have to get back.'

Mary took her nan by the hands. Through the sallow skin and gnarled expression there was a hint of acknowledgment, even love from the old woman. At times it seemed life had drained her of all its joy. Ella had known great hardship and loss, but also love and loyalty. Mary knew inside the cold hard shell was a heart that beat only for those she loved. Mary needed no words to confirm it. She kissed her on the cheek, then hurried across the floor towards the exit. Once gone Ella waited, standing in the centre of the cold, cavernous room. The latch on the door lifted and Ella saw Dot standing in the doorway. Ella spoke.

'It's happening again Dot. I was hoping we'd seen the last of them.'

Dot frowned and nodded.

'The village will never see the last of them. They'll keep coming back for something. They'll keep taking. They always have.'

Ella began to make her way towards the door as she replied.

'It'll be the last we see of them in our lifetime, but I'll be damned if they're taking another from me.'

Ella reached the door and paused by her lifelong friend. Dot gave her a stern look.

'I just hope these younger ones don't forget that. Tolerance is one thing, but they've all gone too soft these days. They haven't seen what we have.'

Ella frowned, and beckoned Dot to follow her.

'Come on. I've said all I need to say on this for now. I've probably said too much. Time's running out for us all.'

The old women left, leaving only the silent echo of their presence. In the far corner of the room there was a long crimson curtain. None of the women had noticed, but at the base of the curtain were two feet. They were bare, with toes protruding, immersed in a small pool of water. The curtain was still, and an eery calm lingered in the room.

14

The storm raged on, showing no sign of easing. Phil, John and Tommy were in the back room at the Railway Inn, not their favourite, but they had been avoiding the Dolphin since Joe had gone missing. It was out of respect for Phil, not wanting to remind him of the incident before he disappeared. There were some that still talked about the events of that evening, implications, but never accusation, leaving others to fill the gaps.

The room was small and smoky, with few lanterns and only scraps of murky light. In one corner was the bar. Little more than a gap in the wall, the drinks would be passed through a hatch in exchange for coins left in a wooden bowl on the counter. The beer was warm, bitter, unpleasant at first, but after a couple no-one noticed or cared. There was a rowdy atmosphere, it was seldom calm. The clamour of colourful conversation jostled with music provided by a rag-tag group huddled round a table in another corner. Most of the songs were old favourites, sea shanties peppered with impromptu folk tunes. Everyone knew the drill, a fiddler would lead the opening bars then someone would pick up the melody, and others would join in. The more popular, up-tempo tunes broke into wild clapping, cheering and hollering, and the stamping of feet. John and Tommy dipped in and out of the revelry, enjoying the playful shanties and drunken camaraderie, but passing on the more melancholy border songs. They cared nothing for the maudlin tunes of death and dishonour, of which there were many. Phil was withdrawn, pensive, preferring to drink in silence. He engaged in the occasional small talk, enough to keep the others happy. Caring little for the music, Phil was only grateful that it provided some distraction to his company, and reason not to natter.

Tommy was up on his feet, clapping and singing, while John joined in from the comfort of his chair. They had drank a few glasses already and John was no longer too steady on his feet. He looked across the table at Phil, staring into his pint glass, pipe in hand, a solemn expression. John shouted across at his friend still clapping and wobbling on the chair.

'What's with you Phil? Come on man.'

Phil forced a smile and took a drink from the glass. Tommy took a seat opposite him. Flush and parched from the merriment, Tommy sank the remainder of his glass, banging it on the table.

'Another?'

Phil shook his head.

'No. I'm alright for now Tommy.'

Tommy went to the hatch, returning with three more glasses filled with ale. He pushed one onto the table towards Phil.

'Here, I got you one anyway. Just in case. What's up Phil? You're not yourself tonight.'

Phil lean back in the seat and sighed. The wooden chair groaned under his weight.

'It's just the past few days Tommy. I think it's catching up with me.'

Phil took a draw on his pipe and puffed smoke into the thick, heavy air. Tommy was a man of many words, but few were best placed for consolation or comfort.

'Aye. There's been a lot happened, but it'll sort itself out. Joe'll turn up and young Tom. You know what kids are like.'

'That's just it Tommy. There's something very odd about the disappearance of young Tom. There were footprints on the beach, they looked like they were heading into the water.'

Tommy took another drink, half-listening, looking over his shoulder, distracted by the music.

'What footprints into the water? You don't think he…You know?'

Tommy nodded at Phil, with an expression that he should know what he meant. Phil frowned.

'No. I doubt he'd do that. I mean he's got a tough life, but he doesn't seem the sort. He's got the girl and he dotes on his mum. He wouldn't abandon her. He was in the boatyard not long since asking me for work, saying he wanted to make a better life for the family. He's a good kid young Tom. No. There's something not right.'

'So what do you reckon?'

Phil picked up his glass and swirled the last of the beer at the bottom before finishing it off.

'I've no idea Tommy. The things is, there were two sets of footprints. Both barefoot and heading for the water. One was definitely a girls. You could see from the size and shape. I thought about a boat, but who'd be stupid enough to launch a boat in this storm? If it wasn't a boat then why were they going into the sea?'

Tommy looked puzzled, grimacing as he shook his head.

'You've got me on that one. There's no lasses gone missing in the village is there? I mean we would have heard. And you're right about a boat. It'd be bloody madness. They wouldn't get very far in this. It's a strange do that's for sure. Let's just hope the footprints have got nowt to do with it. He's probably ran off with some lass he's met.'

There was a commotion a few tables away. A fight had broken out with two men pinning another to the floor while a squat, bearded lad kicked him. The attacker was little more than a boy, but his face was simmering with uncontrolled rage. His kicks were brutal, frenzied, the victim having no chance to defend himself. John had seen enough and launched himself at the two holding the man down. As John tumbled into them, arms flailing, and punches flying, all three men hit the ground and rolled beneath the tables in a heap. Glasses were knocked over and crashed to the floor. The two assailants were beginning to get the better of John, one holding his arms while the other was sneering at him and just about to attack. Tommy joined in, landing a huge blow to the neck of the sneering man. The man buckled, falling to his knees, gripping his throat with both hands, and gasping for air. Tommy then hit the other attacker, in the same place, with the same crippling effect. Tommy stood over the two wounded, fist drawn, waiting for a response, watching as they both choked on the floor. He leant forward and spoke, his voice calm and menacing.

'Now boys. Don't panic, you'll be alright in a while. When you get your breath back you're both going to leave nice and quietly and without any fuss.'

One of the men looked up at Tommy, still gripping his throat, struggling to draw air. His eyes streamed with water as he nodded. Meanwhile, John had turned his attention to the young attacker still crazed, kicking and beating his helpless, now unconscious victim. Grabbing his arm, John dragged the boy away, just as he was about to launch another kick. The young lad went to throw a punch at John, who blocked it and head butted him square in the

The Storm

face. The youngster fell back over the table, more glasses flying everywhere, the crash of them shattering. Rolling across the table, the lad fell crumpled onto the floor alongside his two accomplices.

Meanwhile Tommy was tending the victim who still lay unconscious. The music had stopped as the rest of the bar looked on. Most were excited, hollering in encouragement, a few shook their heads in disapproval. Phil sat perched on the edge of his chair, not amused, but ready to intervene if necessary. He knew Tommy and John meant well. They could handle themselves, and didn't get involved in such matters without good reason.

The original victim was coming round and Tommy and John helped him to his feet. Phil kept an eye on the three attackers as they too struggled to get up. Nursing their wounds and pride, the three young men made their way out of the bar. As Tommy and John sat the victim at their table, the barman began clearing up the mess. Broken glass was spread between overturned tables, swimming in pools of beer. The music began again and soon the room returned to the jovial atmosphere of before, as though the fight had never happened.

Phil sat frowning, looking on as Tommy and John reassured the victim. The man was covered in blood, with several cuts to his face, his eyes and cheeks swollen. Phil didn't know him, and he knew most in the village. Few strangers ventured into this part and those that did more often came as a group looking for trouble. Phil passed the man a glass of ale.

'Here. Have a sup.'

The man shook his head, as Tommy looked at his wounds, wincing as he spoke.

'You're a brave lad coming in here on your own. Those three kids are trying to build a reputation. They're keen, I'll give them that, but they're typical cowards. Three on one is no way to be going on.'

The man struggled to speak, only managing to move the right corner of his mouth and force out a word.

'Thanks.'

There was an odd twang to his words. It may have been the swelling, but Phil thought he had heard the accent before. Tommy spoke.

'No need to thank us mate. We were just making it a bit fairer. That young one doesn't know when to stop. I've seen him on before and he's getting out of hand. I'm going to need to have words with him in the morning. He needs to rein it in before he kills someone.'

John took a long drink and crashed the empty glass on the table.

'Right lads. Are we staying for another, or do we need to get this lad home? Do you live round here?'

The man took a sip from the glass Phil had passed him. His face curled in agony as he swallowed. Phil looked down at the glass, as blood began to twirl mixing with the dark bitter. The man forced out the words again, twisting his face in pain all the while.

'I live up in Ashington.'

John looked at Tommy and frowned. Tommy replied.

'You're from Ashington and you come drinking here!'

The stranger wiped blood from his mouth.

'I've only just moved here. I'm from Ireland. I came over looking for work. They're sinking new coal

The Storm

shafts all the time, and we were told there were plenty of jobs.'

John looked at Phil and Tommy and nodded.

'You're a pitman and you came into this pub. A word of advice: we don't see many folk from Ashington in the village. Those that come don't venture too far into this end, best stick to the west end.'

Tommy smiled and looked across at Phil waiting for a response. Phil frowned as he spoke.

'We're good folk once you get to know us, but there's some you need to watch. Those three are bother, young'uns trying to make a name for themselves. Don't worry, they won't try that again.'

John and Tommy nodded, as the stranger shook his head and held out his hand to Phil.

'Seamus Gallagher. Good to meet you. Sorry, I'm still trying to get my bearings round here.'

Phil took his hand, shaking it with care, as Seamus continued to grimace with pain.

'I'm Phil and this is Tommy and John.'

The men nodded, smiled and shook hands in turn. Phil continued.

'So, are you over here with your family?'

Seamus replied.

'No, my wife and child are still back home in Ireland. The plan is to get settled, then I'l send them the money to get them over.'

Seamus paused, faces and memories flashed through his mind.

'Things are bad back home. This is a new start for us.'

Tommy spoke.

'You're sinking the mine shafts, you say?'

'That's right. It's dangerous, but what's a man to do? You have to take what you can.'

Tommy nodded, before taking a large drink of his ale, and continuing.

'Aye. You're right there Seamus. This whole village was built on danger. There's not a year goes by we don't lose some of our own. The sea's brutal, but we need it to survive. Other than coal there's nothing else round here for the likes of us. I've heard a few folk say that pit work is just as bad, maybe even worse. Can't say I would fancy being stuck underground all day.'

Seamus took a sip, and winced.

'It's not what I would choose to do if I could help it. There's a good many of us don't make it. Sinking is the work no-one wants to do, that's why it's left to us. We're the desperate.'

John and Phil exchanged a knowing glance, as Tommy replied.

'All the best to you and your family. I hope you find what you're looking for here.'

Tommy took Seamus' hand, clutching it with both of his. He then lifted his glass in silent salute and finished off his pint. Slamming the glass down, Tommy got to his feet.

'Now I think it's time we were away.'

Phil stood and helped Seamus to his feet.

'You and John get going and I'll help Seamus up to the narrow path. You lads have done your bit for the night.'

John replied.

'Are you sure Phil? I don't mind helping you.'

'No. It's fine. I can manage. There's no point us all going. You'll be alright making your own way from there Seamus?'

The Storm

Seamus replied.

'Yes, you don't need to come I'll be fine. The night air will do me good.'

Phil shook his head.

'It's no trouble, and I need to be sure they aren't still hanging around waiting for you.'

They all made their way from the bar, shaking a few hands, exchanging words and laughter as they said goodbye to some of the others who would stay on long into the night. Phil headed up the hill towards the outskirts of the village, where a narrow path led to the neighbouring town. This was where the pit shafts were being sunk, and a new community was growing. John and Tommy stumbled in the opposite direction, towards the promenade, meandering down into the dark huddled streets of the fisher end.

As John and Tommy approached the start of the winding street leading to their cottages, Tommy noticed one of the attackers making his way down another lane. It was the young assailant who had been delivering the fierce beating to Seamus. Tommy stopped.

'You go on ahead John, I'll catch you up. I just want to have a few words with that young lad.'

John shook his head and grabbed Tommy's arm.

'Wait Tommy. Just leave it man. There's been enough scrapping for one night. Speak to him tomorrow.'

Tommy pulled his arm free.

'It's alright John. I only want a few words. I won't lay a finger on him. Promise.'

Tommy made off towards the lad, who continued to weave an unsteady route along the cobbled lane. Meanwhile, John set off for home. Approaching the turning into his home street John noticed something move by the door of the lifeboat station. Edging closer, John could see the station door was ajar. He moved towards the door and saw the figure, no more than a shadow, shooting from the darkness and running towards the beach. John could just make out dark clothing and long black hair. It was small, slight and barefoot, but nimble and quick. Reaching the edge of the beach John could see nothing but a veil of darkness, the wind and rain lashing at his face. The tide was high, the waves could be heard smashing against the beach. As his eyes adjusted to the black sky, John could make out the silhouettes of the upturned boats on the far end of the beach. They nestled in silence, just below the church whose spire could be seen stretching into the sky.

John saw the figure again, a movement to his left, someone darting along the prom towards the church, gliding across the sand. John gave chase, the figure taking a sharp left by the church wall and running onto the edge of the moor. John reached the wall and paused for breath. Whoever the shadowy figure was they were too quick for him. Leaning over, hands on his knees, gasping for air, John saw the black silhouette again.

An old wooden hut stood by the far side of the church wall. It had been used as storage for nets and lobster pots, but had fallen into disrepair and been abandoned. John saw the figure waiting just by the entrance to the hut. The shadow paused looked back at him and then moved inside. John crept along the wall, slowing as he neared the door to the wooden building. The door was open, and he eased closer, peering through the crack. Inside the hut was pitch black, there was no movement. John paused and listened, but could hear nothing but the panting of

The Storm

his breath and his heart punching the inside of his chest. After what seemed an age John spoke into the darkness.

'I know you're in there. I'd come out if I was you.'

There was nothing, only darkness and silence. John spoke again, louder this time.

'Come on out. There's no point hiding. You'll have to come out eventually and I'm going nowhere till you do.'

John listened again. There was a movement, someone knocking an object over. The clatter echoed through the darkness. John backed away from the door. Step by step, until he was a good six feet away. All the while he stared at the crack in the doorway, watching and waiting, his breath and heart still pounding. A face appeared, peering through the gap in the door. It was a young woman's face with eyes dark as jade, the purest and deepest pools of night he had ever seen. Her pale white skin was wrapped in long, dark hair that curled like waves around her neck. As she smiled, her face seemed surrounded by an eery translucent glow. The girl reached out her hand, drawing her finger inward, beckoning John to come. John felt his mind drift into a haze, like the rest of the world had dissolved. All he could see were the girl's eyes, her plush red lips and the soft hand urging him toward her. Without thinking or even knowing it, he began to tip-toe towards the girl, edging one footstep at a time, moving ever closer.

John felt a thump on his shoulder as he was hurled to the side onto the wet grass. He rolled over and stared back across at the hut. Through the mist still clouding his mind he saw Tommy standing by the door. His friend had pushed the girl back into the hut and was pushing the door closed. Once the latch was in place, Tommy reached for a long wooden bar on the ground and slammed it down across the door, jamming it shut. John heard screams and yelps from inside the hut, as the girl kicked and banged at the door. It bulged forward as she hammered her body against it, but the bar was thick and strong and held firm. Tommy approached John, crouching on his knees next to him.

'I'm sorry mate. I didn't know what else to do. You seemed in a bit of a trance. Who the hell is she anyway?'

John was still dazed, but was recovering his senses.

'I think I know what she is. There's been talk of them returning. People have been frightened for days now, since the storm arrived. There's been word of sightings and linking it to those that are missing. I thought it was just old women's talk, but whatever's in there, it's not from round here.'

Tommy helped his friend to his feet.

'You wait here and keep an eye on the door. Make sure it doesn't get out. I'm going to get some help. We're going to have to catch it and we'll need more of us. Whatever it is, it's got some strength. Look at the way it's booting that door.'

The door continued to thud and press at the beam with every kick. The yelps and squeals were louder now, more desperate and frenzied. As Tommy set off across the moor and back to the village, John shouted.

'Hurry Tom. I don't think that door will last much longer.'

John crept towards the door, listening to the cries from inside. As he neared, the kicking stopped. There was silence, followed by a low moaning cry. It sounded like weeping, but it was no human sound, it was as though an animal was wounded. John had

The Storm

heard this sound before, but couldn't place where and when. As the crying continued to seep through the cracks in the doorway, John began to pity the creature. It sounded afraid, desperate.

Once again a haze began to wash over his mind. All he could focus on was the sound of the weeping, as his eyes became transfixed on the beam laid across the door. The cries of the creature swirled in his head, and he felt a pain in his chest, a yearning. Something was calling him, compelling him to reach out and lift the beam. John knew he had to free the girl. She was trapped, maybe dying. She needed him.

Lifting his hands, John reached towards the wooden beam. He paused a moment. There was another sound, something washing over the creature's desperate crying, something louder. Through the haze John could hear shouting, a familiar voice. The yearning in his chest began to dissolve and John stepped back from the beam, shaking his head and rubbing his eyes. The shouting had grown louder and John turned to see a group of men heading towards him with torches and lanterns. At the head of the group was Tommy, yelling at his friend.

'Is she still in there John?'

'Yes.'

The frantic kicking began again, and the low, moaning wail was replaced with high pitched shrieks and yelps. The mob approached and huddled round, fizzing with anticipation and excitement. John could hear the men muttering under their breath. He caught flashes of words between the wooshing of the flames from torches, and the desperate cries of the creature trapped within.

'It's one of them. They were right. They're coming for us.'

'It's come to take another. Let's send it back where it belongs.'

'Take no risks Tommy. Be careful lad. Be careful.'

The babble of words grew alongside the tension, as the wailing from the hut reached a frenzied pitch. Suddenly, someone threw a torch onto the roof. John watched as it rolled down, tumbling through a hole in the tiles. There was a loud screech and wild screaming, pained cries and disturbing squeals as the banging and kicking on the door intensified. Another torch was thrown, and another. Soon wave after wave, flame after flame were landing on the roof, all happening in seconds, all too late. John turned to the men.

'Stop it. Stop it now!'

Smoke was billowing through the holes in the roof. Smoke followed by flames. The mob of angry men stepped back. All but John, who looked at the door, and listened to the screams. Once again his eyes were fixed on the wooden beam, all that was preventing the poor creature from escaping, all that stood between life and death. John felt the same strange compulsion rising inside him. The same urge to reach out and remove the beam. John reached for the beam, as Tommy stepped forward and grabbed him.

'What are you doing man?'

'We've got to let her out Tommy. She'll die in there.'

Tommy looked at the door, then up at the flames, now bursting through the roof and high into the air. Smoke was spewing from the windows and the door. The screams were terrifying, and Tommy saw the pity on his friend's face. For a moment Tommy felt the urge for mercy, sharing the urge to free the creature. Then he heard the cries of the mob.

The Storm

'Burn, burn, burn!'

Tommy wrapped his arms round John and dragged him back from the door. John tried to free himself, and though strong and filled with desperation and rage, he was no match for Tommy.

'Let it go mate, let it go. Whatever it is, it got what it deserved.'

As the flames leapt and danced into the stormy sky, the mob looked on. John stopped struggling and dropped to his knees on the long wet grass. He was soaked through, the rain masking the tears running down his face. The screams ended, and the crackle of the fire roared, the flames leaping and dancing as they devoured the wooden building.

There was another sound. This didn't come from the fire engulfing the building, but from behind them, in the distance. This sound came from the sea. It was the same moaning cry they had heard from the girl earlier, a soft, mournful, weeping sound. The cry filled the cloudy sky, sweeping over them like waves on the blustery gusts of wind, falling and rising in volume as it sailed above. Tommy and John looked at each other, then up to the sky. The mob all looked into the darkness, beyond the billowing smoke, and clouds that stretched out in the distance across the moor. As the rain cut their faces and the flames blazed beside them, Tommy and John listened to the cry, to the weeping of the sea.

DAY FOUR

15

A solitary plume of smoke snaked into the thick and heavy morning air, swirling skyward from the charred shell of the old fishing shed. Dense fog hung over the moor, a wall of charcoal grey, while bulging beads of dew clung to blades of fresh grass, sliding, falling, crashing into the dank earth below. The air was damp, mixed with a bitter sting from the smouldering carcass of the hut. A solitary figure stood on the moor, head bowed, surveying all that remained. Gazing at the black stone walls, and burnt splinters of the roof, only the gentle wheeze of his breath could be heard as Phil sucked in the lank and musty air.

Phil approached one of the windows, the boards that had covered it now gone. Peering through the blackened frame, he scanned the smoking rubble that littered the floor. Then Phil saw it, in the far corner. There lay the charred remains of a body, flesh stripped to scorched bone, a gaping mouth locked in terror. Death upon death, tragedy upon tragedy. The storm had brought only pain and suffering and still held them all trapped in its suffocating grip.

Phil left the smouldering remains and made his way along the edge of the wall of the churchyard. The gravestones stood row upon row, in unison, facing the same direction. All except the odd one that looked the other way, a seat in God's kingdom denied, instead an eternity of punishment and shame. Phil reached the end of the wall, where the moor crumbled and met the beach below. He couldn't see the waves for fog, but could hear them as they crashed against the shore. The tide was high, and as he lowered himself onto the deep, heavy sand Phil dragged each step as he moved toward the wetter, firmer beach below.

Phil walked for miles, soaked from the rain, and chilled by the roaring wind, but oblivious to all. The fog enveloped him as he pushed on. Combing the sand all the while, he searched for fragments from the tragedies of days passed, anything the sea had surrendered. Shattered pieces of wood, barrels, pieces of sail, parts of the mast all littered the shore. Bit by bit Phil saw the shattered remnants of the 'Embla'. There were no bodies, no human remains, not even clothes. There was not the slightest sign of the lives the sea had stolen.

As Phil reached the rocks marking the start of the Beacon point, he climbed up onto the edge of the moor. Following the land's natural curve, he made his way round and down towards Lyne burn. He came to the rocky path down the cliff face. It was the same one Peggy had used only days before, the night she came to raise the alarm. At the edge of the burn he saw the waters were high and fast flowing, bursting with days of rain. Phil waited, trapped in two minds as to how to cross. He needed to keep moving, to escape, or at least remind himself he could still escape if he chose to. Phil knew where he was going and who he needed to see.

Following the burn closer to the shore, Phil reached a narrow point where the water splintered and spread before making a final push into the might of the sea. Managing to cross with little trouble, Phil continued along the sand towards his destination. The beach stretched for miles, passed Cresswell and onto Druridge Bay and beyond. Unbroken golden sand that hugged dunes, welcomed the final journeys of rivers, and protected villages all the way up to

Scotland. On a bright summers day there was nowhere better than this burst of God's country, but this was a cold, bleak, windswept winters day. Today god had forsaken them. All majesty and splendour of the beach were shrouded in a veil of grey.

Soon Phil saw the cottages, huts, and fishing boats of Cresswell village. Leaving the beach, he made his way up to the narrow road that weaved between the modest dwellings. The community was much smaller than his own, little more than a few homes hugging a tiny church. He reached the cottage he was looking for, and approached the navy blue door, paint flaking, ravaged by the winter. Phil knocked and waited. The door opened to reveal a tall, burly woman dressed in a bulging dark green dress and dark blue shawl.

'Phil! What a surprise! What brings you here?'

'Can we talk Peggy?'

'Aye. Come in.'

Lowering his head Phil entered the cottage, the warmth of the open fire washing over him, searing the chill from his bones. The room was the familiar layout of his own. Compact and cosy, there was a rickety wooden table, chairs, armchairs and a makeshift kitchen in one corner and a veiled area as a bedroom in another. Peggy took Phil's heavy, sodden jacket and laid it on the back of a chair, shuffling it near to the fire and placing his drenched boots alongside. Phil sat in one of the armchairs by the fire while Peggy busied herself making the customary pot of tea. Rubbing his hands, Phil pressed them close to the flames, stretching his stockinged feet to absorb the comforting warmth. Peggy returned with a laden tray, setting it on a table by the fire. She poured tea, and handed the mug to Phil, preparing another for herself before settling into the other armchair. Satisfied her guest was comfortable Peggy spoke.

'So what brings you here cousin?'

Phil took a sip of tea, and rested the mug on his lap.

'How have things been in the village since the night of the wreck?'

Peggy looked surprised by the question.

'We've been worried about the men. They're still moored up north at Eyemouth and can't get back down, but we've heard they're all safe. Once we got the news we've just settled in and waited for the storm to lift. I've been trying to get on as best I can, but it's a nasty one, isn't it?'

Phil nodded.

'Why'd you ask Phil? I mean why are you really here? It must be important to bring you over in this weather.'

Phil shuffled in the armchair, sitting up and returning his mug to the tray.

'Things haven't been good over our way since the storm arrived. Did you hear about the girl?'

Peggy looked puzzled.

'What girl?'

'I found a survivor from the Embla, a young girl. She was lain on the beach the next morning, half frozen to death. She's staying with us. She's still in shock, and doesn't seem to know where she is, but I think she's OK. She hasn't spoken much since I found her.'

Peggy placed her cup down and leant forward in her chair.

'She's done well to get through that night and survive.'

Phil caught Peggy's eye and the look. He continued.

'I probably found her just in time. She's been lucky.'

'So you found a survivor. That's good, isn't it? What hasn't gone so well?'

Phil continued.

'There've been other things. Incidents. Two of the villagers have gone missing, two young lads. With one of them it could be anything. He's a jack the lad, always up to something, but it's unusual him being away this long without a word. The other lad is different. It's very out of character for young Tom. And the way he disappeared. I don't know, there's something not right about it.'

Phil took another drink of tea, while Peggy eased further forward, now resting on the very edge of her chair. Her face wore a sombre expression.

'You know how it is Peggy. Our generation sees things different, but the old ones, they've been spreading all sorts of tales. There are rumours and whispers and everyone is pointing fingers at the girl. I know who it is.'

Peggy frowned.

'Ella and those other two witches I bet.'

Phil stared at Peggy, his face more serious.

'What is it Phil?'

'You won't have heard.'

'Heard what?'

Phil paused, searching for the words.

'It's Kitty. She passed away.'

Peggy looked shocked, and took a long while to gather her thoughts. All the while Phil looked away, trying to give her space and time. When Peggy spoke, her voice was strained and unsteady with emotion.

'Sorry I didn't know. It wasn't anything linked to the disappearances, or the storm?'

Phil gave Peggy a stern look.

'No. That's already been said, but it's the last thing we need at the moment. Kitty was a good age and the time comes to us all. Don't you start reading stuff into this.'

They sat in silence for a while, as both finished the refreshing tea. Phil demolished the plate of biscuits, washing down the crumbs that stuck to his teeth. Phil broke the silence.

'There is something else. Something serious happened last night.'

His voice tailed away as he lowered his eyes and shook his head. The full force of the night before hadn't really sunk in yet. It wasn't until he had to spell the words out that the incident hit him. Phil coughed, swallowed then forced out the words.

'Some of the men saw another girl in the village, a stranger. John claims she tried to seduce him and she was one of the…'

Phil's voice tailed off for a moment, unable to finish the sentence. After a deep breath, he continued.

'Anyway, John chased her into an old hut on the moor. You know the one by the church wall? A mob turned up, and it all got out of hand. They burnt the hut down with her in it. I've just been there this morning and seen the remains.'

The look of concern on Peggy's face turned to horror. Her mouth was aghast as she lifted her hand to it. Phil avoided her gaze, staring at the floor as he continued.

'I can't get any sense from anyone over there. It's as though the whole village has gone mad. Everyone is on edge, pointing fingers, filling the gaps with superstitious rubbish. Then you've got the old folk stirring it all up, especially Ella and her crew. Last night was the final straw. I just needed to get away, clear my head, talk to someone about it all. I don't know, I'm trying to get my head round everything, make some sense of it.'

There was a long pause, and uncomfortable silence. Phil looked at her, and waited, hoping she would tell him what he needed to hear. But Peggy didn't want to speak. She couldn't find the right words, knew the truth would disappoint him. As the fire crackled in the hearth Peggy spoke, her voice quiet, fragile, on the edge of cracking.

'You know I think the world of you Phil. You're a good, good man, but I know you aren't like this.'

Phil kept staring into the face of his cousin. Those familiar eyes, so often glistening with joy and life were sad, mournful as she reached forward and took his hand.

'You need to get back there. You need to protect each other. You're all in danger.'

The flames of the fire roared up the chimney, a stone exploded and shot onto the rug. Peggy reached down and cast it onto the side of the hearth.

'You know I've little time for superstition, and I don't know who this girl is. Maybe she is a threat, maybe she isn't.'

Peggy paused.

'But the storm, those young men going missing. I know all about this. I've seen it before.'

There was another pause, this time longer.

'There's something else you mightn't have heard, Phil.'

She studied the face of her cousin. He looked tired, drained, far from himself. Peggy knew her words were hurting, but she had to go on.

'The night of the wreck, when the lifeboat came back, there was talk of strange lights and shadows on the rocks. Some of the villagers said they saw creatures, and it was them that took the crew.'

Phil's mind drifted back to the night of the rescue. He recalled what he had seen as they fought to reach the survivors on the rocks. It seemed little more than a dream now, something he had forgotten, that lay buried. Peggy continued.

'There's the storm, the wreck, the lights and creatures. You finding the girl, the deaths and disappearances and the strange girl and the fire. Then, of course, last night. You must have heard it.'

Peggy's voice trembled, as their eyes gripped one another, the tension mixing with the heat, sucking all air from the room.

'Dear lord Phil. You must have. We all heard it.'

The words dissolved as her face filled with panic.

'What?'

'The crying of the sea.'

Phil did hear it. The whole village heard the cries. It and the fire were all anyone spoke of that morning. That was why he had to get away. Peggy took him by the hand.

'Listen you need to get back now. You'll be punished for last night. It won't go unanswered. You need to get everyone indoors and tell them to stay there, especially tonight. They'll be coming.'

Peggy took a deep breath.

'Is anyone with child?'

Phil was silent, his face blank. Peggy shook his hand and spoke again, her voice louder, her words more pronounced.

'Is anyone with child Phil?'

The words hit him again, as Mary's face filled his mind. His wife's beauty was gone, her eyes bulging with fear, her mouth wide open as she forced a silent scream. Phil felt his heart pounding as the adrenalin and panic began to build.

'Yes. Why?'

'That's why they come Phil. They come for the young men and the unborn. Don't you remember the rhyme and the stories when we were kids? You must remember it?'

The faint words of a rhyme began to echo inside Phil's head. They were distant words, sung in innocence, backed by the sweet, playful melody of a child. One by one the words assembled and took shape. Words he had buried, now resurfaced, crawling from the darkest furrows of his mind. They rolled over and over in his head, backed by the lilting tune.

'Dark girl, strange girl
Where is't that you do come?
Beware the sons of fishermen
For the sea is where I'm from

Dark girl, strange girl
Why is't that you do cry?
I am longing for family
In dark water they do lie'

There was something missing, lost or stolen. More words bubbled from somewhere deep inside, the missing verse, locked in the cellars of his mind all these years. It was a verse the children were told never to sing, only to remember. Words, if recited they would be punished for. Phil had an image of Sunday school and the stern face of a much younger Ella bellowing at him for singing the verse. She warned him never to utter those words again, and never to say their name. To do so was to invite them in. The lost verse came and cast the other two aside, rattled like a drum inside. Over and over. Again and again.

Dark girl, strange girl
What mischief is't you make?
Beware I am the Selkie
Your unborn babes are what I'll take'

....

Phil trudged across the sand with heavy, determined strides, oblivious to the chaos around him. The mist continued to smother him as the time edged into late afternoon. The few fragments of light that had managed to seep through were receding. Somewhere the sun was dissolving into a horizon, another day unseen. The chill in the wind was biting harder now. Phil pressed on, anxious to get back, fuelled by the fire of Peggy's words. Desperate to return to Mary.

Moving across the sand Phil slowed and stopped as something caught his eye. It was a few feet in front, on the edge of the shoreline, where the waves had not long since stroked the sands. As he edged forward Phil saw the clothing first, then shoes, and the hair. He approached the body, stood over it, as the crash of the waves melted away. All Phil could hear was the pounding of his heart and heaving of his gasping breath. It was as though he was underwater, the only sounds now echoing from within. Phil couldn't see the face, he didn't need to. He recognised the clothes and hair.

16

Maggie's wailing and screaming filled the room, as her fists pounded down on Phil's chest, tears streaming down her face. Locked in the futile anger of heartache and despair the other women dragged Maggie away, and lay on the bed with her. Phil heard them whispering words of comfort as they rocked the widow like a newborn. The screams eased and faded into whimpers of anguish, as Phil looked on helpless. He hadn't wanted to be the one to tell Joe's young wife, but he had no choice. Phil had found the body. He had carried it back across the beach and moor, taken it to the lifeboat house and laid it out on the table. It was he who had covered it in a blanket to hide Joe's face, the expression frozen in terror, the eye sockets gorged leaving only gaping, empty holes.

After mumbling another sorry and goodbye, Phil slipped out of the door. No-one noticed. All eyes were on Maggie, trying to calm and comfort her, ease the shock and sorrow. Maggie and the baby, Joe's unborn child. Phil made for home, head bowed, his mind still numb. The tortured look on the young man's face flashed into his head, jostling with the screams of his widow. Phil winced as he felt a cold spear of pain and grief shoot through him. Then there was Mary, her warm smile gone, replaced with lines of worry and concern. His wife's image faded and he saw the girl, looming over him. Her head moved towards him, and he felt her warm lips touch his, tasting her sweet breath. As Phil's eyes closed there was only darkness, the touch and taste lingering within. He shook the daydreams from his head and concentrated on the cobblestones, as he marched towards home.

He was almost there when he saw her. She was standing at the top of the street, at the edge of a stone wall, a gas lamp draping her in its eerie glow. Phil stopped, but Ellie didn't move, just stood and stared, as always. Then his daughter turned and ran, around the corner, off down the meandering streets. Phil followed her and as he reached the place where she had stood caught a glimpse of her darting down an alley. Reaching the entrance to the alley, Phil saw her waiting at the far end, watching his every move. He edged his way forward, but as he neared she bolted. For several minutes they continued this cat and mouse - father and daughter, playing games down familiar lanes and alleys. As they had done so many times before. They continued until they reached the promenade, then onto the gates of the church. There the little girl paused again before heading into the churchyard.

Phil reached the gates, and searched inside for his daughter. The graveyard was covered in a thick blanket of mist and darkness, she was nowhere to be seen. Then Phil heard a voice, a cry, the weeping of a small child echoing from the depths of the mist. He walked towards the sound, as it disappeared. He waited, listened, but there was only the whistling of the wind between the graves and the patter of rain on the cobbled path. The crying came again, louder this time and to his left. Phil stepped between the gravestones towards the cry, realising where he was heading, where the cry was coming from. An icy chill ran through him. He stopped, faltered, was caught in two minds whether to go on. This was a place he had been only once before, and had vowed never to return. Phil turned and headed back towards the gates, as the cry evaporated in the mist behind him. It ended just as he reached the gates. Pausing for a moment, Phil stared back across the graveyard. He saw nothing. Phil knew she was there though. They all were, and always would be.

As Phil burst through the door, he hurled his jacket onto the table, and collapsed into the armchair. Mary stood at the other side of the table, drying dishes. She lowered the plate, placing it by the sink, then shuffled towards her husband. Phil looked up and spoke as she approached.

'How is she?'

'Devastated. What do you expect?'

His eyes were vacant, and mind still swamped with flashing images and sounds.

'The poor girl. They had so much to look forward to.'

Mary's eyes were fixed on her husband.

'And how are you?'

Phil wanted to lie, but there was no point. Mary knew and read him. There were no secrets. Shaking his head, Phil looked up into her soothing eyes.

'What's happening Mary? What the hell is going on?'

Mary moved towards the fire, as the flames roared and the coal crackled and spat, her gentle whisper could only just be heard.

'I don't know. I really don't, but it needs to end.'

Phil's voice was little more than a soft whisper too, careful not to disturb the girl.

'I went to see Peggy this morning. She thinks we're in danger.'

'She's not the only one. There are many others saying it too.'

Mary turned to face Phil.

'You need to get everyone together, talk to them, reassure them, work out what we're going to do. They'll listen to you.'

'What do you mean what we're going to do?'

Mary frowned.

'We need to do something Phil. We can't just sit around and wait. We're prisoners in the village, just waiting for it to happen.'

'For what to happen?'

Mary shouted.

'For Christ's sake Phil, there's something not right and you know it. Everyone does.'

Phil looked alarmed, both by Mary's anger and for fear the girl might hear. He gestured towards the corner and the bed behind the veil. Realising his concern Mary calmed herself, and lowered her voice.

'And what about her?'

'What about her?'

Mary paused.

'We're going to have to do something with her. I don't want her in the house any longer.'

Phil sat forward in the chair.

'What are we supposed to do with her?'

'I don't want her staying here. Speak to someone and see if there's somewhere else she can stay until the storm lifts. As soon as it does, get her back where she belongs.'

Phil cupped his hands and pressed them against his forehead, banging them, as he grimaced with despair.

'Dear God, not you as well. I thought you were better than that.'

Mary stepped forward. Leaning over she pressed her face close to his, her voice still a whisper, but fizzing with anger.

'I can't take any chances Phil. We can't. There's too much at stake now. It's not just about us anymore.'

There was a long pause as her words echoed in his head. Then the words of the rhyme crept in, echoing in Phil's mind. There were just a few words, 'your unborn babes are what I'll take' repeating over and over, mingled with Peggy's warning, 'that's why they come Phil. They come for men and the unborn'. Could the girl have something to do with all this? Was she really one of them? Had he brought danger into his community, and his own home? Phil's mind was swirling with all that had happened, overlain with images of Mary, the girl, and Joe's dead body. Wave after wave of pictures rolled through his head. He felt ill, confused and exhausted. He wanted the thoughts to stop, the storm, the disappearances, the deaths, the pain, the heartache, the whispers, the suspicion. It was time for everything to end. Phil looked down at Mary, her eyes simmering with anger.

'I'll speak to the vicar. We'll get everyone together in the morning.'

Phil took a moment before continuing.

'You're right. This has gone on long enough.'

'And the girl?'

Mary waited for Phil to reply, with only the roar and crackle of fire filling the silence of the room.

....

Maggie lay on her side sleeping, her brow peppered with tiny beads of sweat. Her breathing was heavy, laboured, as her chest pressed against a bulging stomach. Inside the baby kicked, its tiny hand pressed against the wall of Maggie's womb. The unborn child's movements became more frenetic, as it struggled. Locked behind a wall of skin, submerged in a sea that imprisoned and protected, it could feel the eyes. They were watching over Maggie and her unborn. The darkest eyes, like the purest jet washed upon the shore. Wave after wave crashing and polishing the stone, across oceans of time.

The creatures stood at the foot of the bed, two of them, emitting the same translucent glow. Their long dark hair nestled on black gowns, faces painted in sinister pleasure. They waited, watching Maggie's chest as it filled with air, then compressed again, a slow rhythmic movement, the pulse of life. Their eyes burnt holes through Maggie as she slept, penetrating skin and sea, stabbing at the child within, the unborn child, their prize. The creatures watched the widow's eyelids flicker as she dreamt. Buried deep in the crevices of her mind, she was drowning in sleep, fathoms below, anchored to the ocean floor. Gentle waves ebbed and flowed, soothed her, washed away the demons of the waking world. Maggie was at peace, unaware of the threat to her and the unborn child. The baby continued to wrestle and fight. It wasn't dreaming. It was awake, blind in sight, but seeing all that was coming, frantic but unable to break free. The child was trapped in a tomb of water.

The baby felt the creature's fingers press against the stomach wall, stroking the skin, then prodding and poking. They eased Maggie onto her back, careful not to wake her, lost in waves of dreams. They laid her legs out straight and lifted her nightgown. She lay naked before them, the mound of stomach exposed, the delicate wall of skin all that lay between them and what they had come for. One of the creature's looked on, a flash of delight etched on her lips. The other raised its hand, a blade hovering just above Maggie's skin. The baby sensed the ice cold metal as it caressed its mother, sliding across the surface, gliding like a child on a frozen lake. The baby's tiny, fragile heart was pounding, while Maggie lay motionless, locked in their spell.

The blade stopped, point poised, pressed just against the wall of the womb. The creature waited, squeezing out the final moments of pleasure, the seconds before, when everything was still to come. Their prize, the unborn child.

DAY FIVE

17

Beth lay screaming and sobbing on Phil and Mary's bed, as Mary tried to comfort her. She was hysterical, babbling, and making little sense. Meanwhile, the girl sat at the bottom of the bed, poised on the edge, rocking back and forward, hands covering her ears, mumbling to herself. Ella looked on, a bitter scowl carved in her face, thrusting daggers at the girl. Leaning over, Phil tried to pick out fragments of Beth's words, looking confused and helpless. He stared at Ella.

'What happened?'

The expression on Ella's face didn't change, as she spoke.

'They came for her. I knew they would.'

'What did you see?'

The old woman shook her head.

'I didn't see them, I didn't have to. I only saw what they left behind and what they took.'

Phil turned to face her, standing up straight, towering over the tiny frame of Ella. His voice boomed, unable to contain his anger.

'Just tell me what happened, will you?'

Ella took her time, as she looked down at Mary and Beth. Her granddaughter cradled Beth in her arms as she sobbed. The girl rocking back and forth, staring into nowhere, her eyes lifeless. Ella looked up at Phil who stood over her, eyes ablaze. When she was ready Ella spoke.

'They were always going to come. They want the unborn. They always do. That's why they come. It was only a matter of time. Beth found Maggie this morning. She went to wake her and saw what they'd done.'

Ella paused.

'They took the child.'

Phil placed his hand on his head, turned and began to pace the room.

'How? I don't understand.'

'They came in the night while Beth and Maggie were sleeping. They cut Maggie open and took the child. The creatures are cold, heartless. They'll stop at nothing to get what they want. I warned you Phil, but you wouldn't listen.'

Phil stopped pacing, stared back at Ella, his expression a mix of horror and anger.

'What? They just cut her open.'

'Yes Phil. Maggie's dead and the child has gone.'

Phil plunged into a chair and put his head in his hands. His whole body shook as he beat his fists on the arm of the chair. He let out a blood curdling cry seething with anguish and pain. The others were shocked. Mary looked up and spoke as she continued to cradle Beth.

'Phil. We need to get everyone together. They need to be warned. We have to put a stop to this now.'

Phil continued to shake, still drowning in guilt and despair. Rubbing his face with his hands, unable to believe all he had known was crumbling. Ella and Mary looked on, waiting. Mary barked at him.

'Come on Phil. We need to get going. Now!'

Mary's anger was the trigger that shook him from his stupor. Looking dazed and jaded, Phil rose to his feet. He gazed round the room, gathering his thoughts before speaking.

The Storm

'Ella, can you go and round people up. Tell them to meet at the church hall. Mary, you stay here with Beth and the girl.'

Phil gave Mary a knowing look. His wife nodded as Ella made her way to the door. Just as the old woman was about to leave Phil shouted after her.

'Ella. Please, I need you with me on this.'

The old woman turned and left without a word. Phil looked at Mary.

'I'm going to Maggie's and then I'll go and get the vicar. Wait here. I'll come and get you after the meeting.'

Phil grabbed his coat and left. Oblivious to the fury of the storm, he darted through the cobbled streets towards Joe and Maggie's cottage. Soon there, he approached the door pausing for a moment before entering. Easing the door open, the room was bathed in darkness, the curtains still drawn. The only light was from a few dying embers in the fireplace. The black, empty silence was suffocating. Phil found a candle, lit it and edged towards the veil in the corner of the room, beyond which was the bed. Creeping forward, he bumped into the leg of a chair. The sound of the wood scraping across the stone floor echoed around the tiny room. Reaching the veil, Phil paused, watching the light from the candle as it flickered against the white sheet, and cast strange shadows upon it. Phil reached out and peeled back the sheet.

It was Maggie's face he noticed first. Eyes and mouth closed, her expression was locked in quiet serenity at odds with the terrible injuries below. There was no indication of trauma, or struggle. It was as though she were unaware of all that had happened, her life drained from her, and the unborn child taken.

Even in the faint glow of the candlelight Phil could see the blood. There was a clear and clean incision across her lower stomach, the wound from which the child within had been snatched. Other than that, they left no trace. There was no weapon. Nothing. Only the horror remained.

Bowing his head, Phil whispered a prayer. As his lips formed the words, he thought of young Joe and the mutilated body that lay in the lifeboat station waiting to be prepared for burial. Now he would be joined by his young bride. She too had a life of hope and promise ripped from her along with that of their unborn child. Everything the young couple had to live for. All they had looked forward to was gone. Taken, stolen from them. Phil thought of the girl, his daughter Ellie, her angelic features, and radiant smile. It was the first time he had recalled an image of her smiling face in a long time. He heard her voice as she called to him, laughing, singing and skipping across the golden sands of the bay. It was a hot summer's morning and they were both making their way to the boatyard. It was the day that held so much joy, and ended as though the world itself was over. A part of the world died that day, along with a piece of Phil. He gazed down at Maggie's body, her legs pressed together, toes pointed out straight. She was at peace, her arms laid across her chest, ready to move on, wrapped in a veil of blood.

Anger filled Phil, so much he could taste it. Stepping from behind the veil, he moved to the door. Turning and taking one last look around the room, Phil blew out the candle and left. He scrambled across the slippery cobbles, along the sand drenched prom and on to the church. As he entered Phil saw the vicar standing on the pulpit, face down, reading something. Matthew looked up as he heard Phil approaching, his heavy footsteps echoing around the cavernous chamber.

'What is it Phil?'

Phil's steps were brisk and determined, his face flustered.

'Father, I need you to come quickly to the church hall. We're rounding up the villagers. We need to speak with everyone.'

Sensing the urgency, the vicar jumped down from the pulpit, grabbed his coat and approached Phil.

'What is it Phil? What's happened?'

Gasping for air, Phil paused as the vicar looked on, his face grave with concern. Phil caught his breath and spoke, his voice booming in the empty chancel.

'There's been another death.'

Phil paused.

'It's Maggie.'

Horror swept across Father Matthew's face.

'No! How? I mean, dear God.'

The vicar looked up and made the sign of the cross, as Phil continued.

'She was murdered in the night, while she was sleeping. Beth was with her the whole time and heard nothing. They've gotten in and taken…'

Phil stopped, unable to form the words, unsure what it was he had to say. Father Matthew looked on, watching Phil's lips, waiting for him to continue.

'What is it Phil?'

'They took the child.'

The vicar's look of horror melted into bewilderment. There was a long silence while he processed the words, tried to make sense of what Phil had said.

'I don't understand. How could they have taken the child?'

The realisation hit Matthew, the full impact of all that had been said. Images flashed through his head, bombarded him, macabre pictures of things he had not seen, didn't need to see. Then there were voices, whispers and rumours, things he had overheard. The words filled his mind, as the vicar spoke.

'So it's true. They're here. First the ship's crew, then Joe, Tom and Kitty, now Maggie and her child.'

Matthew paused, pacing in a circle, looking at the stone floor and shaking his head.

'We must have angered them.'

There was another silence as the vicar continued to pace. Phil looked on, as the vicar continued.

'It was the fire the other night, the burning of that girl. She was one of them and they want us to pay for it. That's it. This must be their retribution, our punishment.'

Phil interrupted.

'None of us know what's going on, but we're in danger. We need to stick together, look out for each other. Ella's rounding folk up in the church hall. We need to act, and we need a plan. We can't go on like this. There won't be any more deaths.'

The fisher folk were gathering. Ella had spread the word and it rippled through the narrow streets like the energy building in the waves. As Phil and the Father headed along the cobbled lanes people were leaving their homes. Wrapped in thick coats, hats and shawls, the villagers were braving the unwelcoming intensity of darkness and storm. All were making their way towards the church hall, filled with curiosity, excitement, and fear. None knew how the day would end.

18

The hall was rumbling with the cacophony of babble and chatter. Already packed, fishermen, women, and children were still arriving from the neighbouring streets. A tension hung over everyone, mingled with the damp, musty air and simmering glow of candles and lamps dotted around the room. People sat on wooden benches, laid out in crooked rows, order in the midst of chaos. Ella sat at the front, arms folded, head forward, waiting, ignoring the din around her. Dot entered, surveyed the room and made her way to sit beside her old friend. Men huddled at the back of the room, puffing pipes, and speaking in soft, agitated whispers. Women lined the benches, locked in animated conversation while their children played alongside, oblivious to the danger, but excited by this unexpected drama.

All eyes turned to Phil and Father Matthew as they entered the hall. The chatter quietened and stopped as both men made their way to the front. The vicar removed his overcoat and hat, brushing off the water, as he laid them on a chair. His face was pink and raw, his expression and mood sombre. Phil faced the crowd, still in his thick winter garments, his huge presence filling the room. Father Matthew moved alongside Phil, stepped forward, raised his hands and spoke.

'Thank you everyone for coming. I know you must be wondering why we've called you all here, so we'll get straight to the point.'

The vicar paused to clear his throat, as the light and shadows cast an eery glow on him in his white robes.

'You will know of the disturbing events in the village these past few days. Firstly, the tragedy of the shipwreck and two of our young men disappearing. Then there was poor Kitty, and the fire on the moor two nights ago. Some of you will no doubt know one of the missing men, Joe Arkle, was washed up on the beach yesterday.'

The vicar looked at Phil whose head was bowed. Amongst the people who had gathered there was a flurry of whispers and movement. Most knew of Joe, but to some the other events were a shock. The Father waited for everyone to settle before continuing.

'It would now appear there has been further tragedy last night.'

The vicar waited, scanned the many familiar faces in the crowd as they glared at him, hanging on each word, urging him to go on.

'Joe's wife Maggie was found dead this morning.'

Huge gasps swept through the hall, as all order collapsed and everyone erupted in a flurry of alarmed discussion. All the while Ella and Dot sat facing forward, no expression on their faces, no emotion. One of the men at the back stood and spoke, shouting above the noise.

'How did it happen Father?'

Matthew raised his hands again, trying to calm everyone down, restore some order. He waited for people to stop, letting them release the shock and tension. Once the noise began to ease the vicar looked back at the man and replied.

'We don't know Robert. Or at least we can't be sure yet.'

A voice shouted from the other side of the room.

'Was she murdered?'

The Storm

The conversations erupted again, charged with emotion, mixed with exclamations of shock. Matthew waited, as waves of fear and nervous energy swept through them once again. Phil stepped forward, standing up tall and shouting above the din, his booming voice brushing the chatter aside. All eyes turned to Phil and the room fell quiet again.

'I know this is a shock to you all, but please hear us out.'

The room fell silent, all eyes focused on Phil. It was now so quiet they could hear the whistling of the wind through the rafters and the heavy patter of the rain on roof and windows. Phil scanned the faces of the crowd, so many friends and family, all known since he was a child. They had nursed and watched him, taught and scolded him, now they were all looking to Phil for answers. He would tell them what to do and they would follow.

Phil's mouth felt dry, filled with a sour taste. Composing himself, he addressed the people again.

'We can't be sure what happened to Joe and Maggie, but until we find out we need to be wary and on our guard. We need to stick together as a community, and look out for each other. That is what we do best, and now more than ever we need to be there for each other.'

Another voice from the group spoke. It was a woman nestled in the midst of the crowded benches.

'Is it safe to leave our houses?'

Phil felt her gaze, saw her fear.

'Just go home, lock your doors and stay there. Don't leave the house unless you have to, especially at night. Be especially careful at night.'

Another woman shouted from the back of the room.

'It's them, isn't it? They've come because of the fire. It's revenge. The girl that burned was one of them, wasn't she?'

Noise erupted again, as Phil and the vicar tried to calm everyone. Phil shouted above the din.

'Just settle down, can we?'

They waited as the flurry of anger and fear began to subside.

'I know there's been a lot of rumours about what's going on. I've heard all the tales. I doubt anything I say here is going to change the minds of some of you. I know these superstitious stories run deep. We've been told them since we were kids and it's hard to know what's true and what's just fairy tale. Let's just stick to what we do know. We're in danger and as of yet we don't know who from. We need to stick together, watch out for each other until the storm lifts. Then we can seek help from town.'

Ella spoke.

'What if the storm doesn't lift Phil? What if it's here for a reason? What if it won't go until they get what they're after?'

The old woman glared at Phil, her voice strained, the passion bringing her close to tears. Phil waited before answering, his voice calm, concealing the anger inside, and his disgust at her public show of disloyalty.

'It's all 'what ifs?' Ella. There's a lot we don't know, but all this superstition is doing no-one any good.'

The wind whistled and the rain rattled outside, as all eyes fixed on Phil. He scowled at Ella, wanting to continue to expose the pettiness of her superstitions, crush her blindness and prejudice. Phil knew this was not the time or place. Father Matthew stood alongside, head bowed. Sensing the moment was right to smother this before it got out of hand the vicar spoke.

'Everyone please, just do as Phil says. Go to your houses, lock your doors, and stay inside at night. All we care about is your safety. There has been too much suffering and we will do all we can to see there is no more.'

The vicar surveyed the sea of faces, many now looked down. He could see the anguish, felt their pain, and only wanted to take it away from them.

'Before we go, let us join together in prayer.'

All heads lowered and the room was bathed in silence, still simmering with the energy of fear. Father Matthew bowed his head and began to utter the opening lines of the prayer.

'Our Father, who art in Heaven'

The voice of the vicar echoed around the room, the words reaching out to them all. Each heart was pumping, fuelled with fear, pondering the events of the past few days. Mothers held their children closer, while fathers raged with violent thoughts. The rhythm of the every day had been ruptured, living now filled with terror and anger. There was poison in the veins of the village, a suspicion that needed to be cured before it consumed them all. Father Matthew brought the prayer to a close.

'Amen. May the Lord watch over and protect each and every one of us. Now go to your homes and stay safe. We'll let you know when things change. God bless us all.'

Chatter erupted as though a lid had been lifted. Some got to their feet and made for the door, others huddled in seats and exchanged worried looks. Ella and Dot stood, all the while Ella's eyes were fixed on Phil. He approached the old women, his face grave.

'You shouldn't have done that Ella. It could have been said elsewhere, not in front of everyone.'

Phil waited for a response, but Ella lowered her head. He continued.

'You've been stirring enough trouble as it is. Whatever you think, we're still family and some things are best discussed in private.'

Ella shook her head and spoke, her voice soft and calm.

'Maybe you're right Phil. I'm sorry, but I'm not the one who's brought one of them into the family.'

Phil frowned.

'What do you mean one of them?'

'The girl you saved. Do you think anyone could survive a night in that sea or on the beach? You said she was naked when you found her. Come on Phil. You know the truth. She's one of them. She's a Selkie. As long as she's here you're putting all of us in danger. Think about Mary. Hasn't she been through enough?'

Phil heard Ella's words as a song filled his head. It was the voice of a child, a rhyme, a familiar melody from the past. It was the forbidden verse, with the word they were warned to never speak, the name that invited them in.

Dark girl, strange girl
What mischief is't you make?
Beware I am the Selkie
Your unborn babes are what I'll take'

The song dissolved, but the name hung in the air - Selkie, Selkie, Selkie. Phil stared at Ella, as he towered over the tiny old woman. Her face was twisted in a gnarled scowl.

The Storm

'Take your wicked tongue and sad ways and go. You're a bitter old woman, and what you don't understand, you just fill with your superstition and hatred.'

Phil's voice was cracking, his rage close to bursting. Ella spat out her reply.

'No the problem is you don't understand. You may think I'm a bitter old fool, but I've lived three times the life you have, seen things you wouldn't even imagine. Yes, that thickens the skin, but it also teaches you to be wary, especially when it comes to your own.'

There was a pause as Ella took a deep breath.

'You're a good man Phil. Everyone respects you, even me. You may not think it, but I do. But your goodness blinds you, makes you weak. You don't see what's really happening. You don't want to, you won't let it, you don't want to see the evil in the world, you don't believe it's real. But it's everywhere, if you care to look. And now it's in your own home. Even Mary sees it.'

Those final words stung him like tiny daggers. Ella hurled them at him one by one, even her love and respect couldn't contain the urge to attack. Phil felt both women's burning eyes upon him. He wanted to unleash all his anger upon them, but began to wither instead as the words sunk in.

'Even Mary sees it.'

What did she mean? What had been said between them? Was everyone against him, even those he loved the most? Phil bit his lip, and clenched his fists. His heart was racing, as he tried to compose himself. When he spoke his voice was quieter, in part to contain the anger, but also beaten by Ella's poisonous words.

'Stay away from me and Mary. You're no longer welcome in our home.'

Phil pushed past the old women, and nudged his way through the people preparing to leave. He stormed out of the hall, slamming the door behind.

....

'Can we talk?'

Mary could see her husband was angry. Beads of sweat clung to his brow, he was out of breath, and soaked through.

'What is it Phil?'

Beth and the girl lay sleeping on the bed, Mary was on the floor by their side, leaning over, stroking Beth's hair. Mary got to her feet, and moved towards Phil who remained standing by the door.

'What is it love?'

Phil looked down at the floor. His throat was dry, as his voice wrestled to hide his emotions.

'I've just spoken to Ella. She was at her wicked best.'

His head remained bowed, as he mumbled through his beard.

'She warned me again, about the girl. She thinks I'm putting us all in danger.'

Mary fumbled with her hands in the pockets of her dress, as Phil waited for a response. It was clear his wife wasn't ready to speak.

'She thinks I'm blinded by my nature, that I'm too concerned with helping others. That I'm a fool for not seeing what the girl really is, that I'm the only one who can't see it. The only one!'

Mary moved towards him, reaching out and touching his arm.

'I spoke to her the other day. We talked about the girl. I'm sorry I should have told you.'

Phil yanked his arm away, looked up, glaring at his wife. His voice was raised, seething in anger.

'It's bad enough trying to fight the lies and suspicion in this place without finding out you're in on it too.'

'It wasn't like that. All I said was how difficult it'd been with all three of us in the house. I asked if she could find someone else who would take the girl for a few days. Just till the storm lifts.'

Phil began pacing back and forward as Mary continued.

'I'm not sure about all this talk about her. Maybe it is just old wives tales.'

Mary paused and clutched her stomach.

'But I don't want to take any risks with the baby.'

As she stroked her abdomen, Mary looked up at Phil who frowned, fighting to keep it together.

'You didn't tell Ella about the baby, did you?'

'No! I've told no-one. Only we know, and the girl.'

Phil stopped pacing. Looking back at the veil, he moved towards Mary, pressing his face close to hers.

'The girl?'

'Yes, the girl. The other day we were alone and she touched my stomach and said baby.'

A grave look spread across Phil's face.

'What? She said that?'

Phil looked lost, deep in thought. Mary touched his shoulder.

'Look Phil, I know why you're trying to save the girl. You want to make up for what happened. But you can't. Nothing can ever make up that.'

Phil fought back the tears as Mary continued, her voice growing as the emotions swelled inside her.

These were words she should have said a long time ago, conversations avoided, buried in simmering blame and anger.

'You think the more people you save, the more it'll make things better, but you'll never bring her back Phil. We've lost her. She's gone.'

Phil lowered his head, rocking back and forth, tears streaming down his cheeks. Mary looked on, her eyes glistening in the faint, shimmering light. The couple stood awhile, lost and alone, neither able to let go. Mary lifted her arm and began to reach out her hand towards her husband. She paused, just before they touched. Phil spoke, his voice cracked, shattered with emotion.

'You're right. When I look at the girl I see Ellie. That day I found her on the beach she looked so lost and helpless. At first I thought it was her. I so wanted it to be her.'

Phil took a moment, swallowing and wiping away the tears.

'She was lying there in a ball, just like Ellie did. It was as though the sea had returned her, as if it was giving her back.'

Mary gazed at her husband, tears falling as she whispered.

'She isn't coming back Phil. It's time to move on'

Their eyes locked, sorrow and resignation. After a long silence Phil spoke.

'I'll make this right. I promise.'

Mary sighed and nodded, as her husband continued.

'I'm not sure what's going on, but I'll find out. I'll make sure no harm comes to you or the baby.'

Phil looked down at Mary's stomach. Their future lay within, somewhere beyond the thin wall of protection was a tiny piece of life that would grow and grow. Life within life, joy within joy. The endless circle. All that he loved was standing before him and Phil knew he would do anything to protect them.

....

The girl slipped into the night, leaving Phil, Mary and the others sleeping. The streets were desolate, the darkness and ravages of the storm had sucked all life from the village. Just a few days before the lanes had been bustling with joy and laughter, as children played, and people chatted. Now they were gone, only black clouds, wind and rain remained. The storm had come and piece by piece stripped each layer of life from the community. The storm and the Selkie had arrived, taken what they wanted, and would return for more.

Dressed only in a few flimsy clothes, the girl's feet were bare. Tears streamed down her face as she approached the rocket house standing at the rear of the lifeboat station. A small, stone building, it took its name from the small, crude missile fired from shore to sea to assist those stranded in the water. The missile was a last resort, used only when the seas were too treacherous for the lifeboat to be launched. The rocket had saved many lives, tonight it would shelter another.

Two large wooden doors stood at the front of the building, but the girl entered a small door at the side. The damp, musty room was wrapped in a blanket of darkness, the floor littered with an array of apparatus that the girl tip-toed around. She reached the back wall, leant against it, shivering, hugging herself, trying to cling to the remaining fragments of warmth. The girl slid down the wall and sat crouched on the stone floor. Rocking back and forth, weeping and alone.

19

'She's gone!'

Phil stood over the bed, Mary, Beth and John standing by his side. Beth was rubbing her eyes and shaking her head. She spoke.

'She was lying next to me. I didn't hear her leave.'

Phil paced the room, Mary looked on while John comforted his wife. Mary spoke.

'She can't have gotten far Phil.'

Grabbing his coat, Phil made for the door.

'Wait here. I'm going to look for her. If she comes back before me just wait here. Don't leave the house!'

John stood up, and took his coat.

'I'm coming with you. We've more chance if we split and look for her.'

Phil was standing by the open door.

'No. You stay here and watch these.'

Mary stood and moved towards them, ushering both men to leave. John barged past Phil and out into the street. Mary kissed Phil on the cheek.

'Both of you go. We'll be fine. I promise we won't leave.'

Phil smiled, his face a mixture of love and worry. As he turned to leave he gave one last command.

'Lock the door behind me.'

The two friends stood in the dark street, huddled close. John awaited instructions, as Phil weighed up their options. Soon Phil spoke.

'You take the lanes to the right, I'll go left. We'll zig-zag our way down and I'll meet you at the bottom outside the lifeboat station. If she doesn't turn up we'll split up and take ends of the beach and prom. OK?'

'Fine by me. Don't worry Phil, she'll turn up.'

Phil put his hand on John's shoulder and frowned.

'I hope you're right. I just pray we find her before someone else does, or no-one has taken her already. If anyone has, they'll wish they hadn't.'

Phil's angry words hung in the air. Phil was a man of honour, but he was not to be crossed. Remain loyal and you had a friend for life. Betray him and you faced a formidable enemy.

John patted his friend on the back, then darted into the darkness down the street to the right. Phil looked on as the shadow disappeared from view. He set off down another lane, snaking in the opposite direction. The lantern was held high above his head, guiding his way through the claustrophobic blackness. All the while Phil's eyes were peeled, scouring every nook, where shadows concealed shadows. Weaving his way through the tunnels of night, he fought the stinging spray of swirling wind and rain. Not a soul walked the streets. Not even the spirits of the dead dared come out on this night. Phil reached the bottom of the lane and waited by the lifeboat station. Standing in the shelter of a small roof, he huddled close to the side entrance of the rocket house. Watching and waiting, Phil searched the darkness for any sign of John or the girl.

There was a clatter from inside the rocket house, something falling to the floor. Phil leant into the door and listened, but there was nothing. Gripping the handle and turning till it clicked, Phil teased the door ajar. He slipped the lantern through the gap in the door and peered in.

'Is anyone there?'

There was no reply as the golden hue of his lamp reached inside, too weak to light the whole room. Phil edged through the door, as it creaked and groaned. Tip-toeing along the bench on the back wall, he noticed a hammer lying on the floor. He stopped, listened, ears burning in the deafening silence, reaching out to find any trace of sound. Then he heard it, a quiet whimpering, the faint intermittent crying of a child. Phil edged towards the sound, lantern held out front, sweeping away each layer of darkness as he crept across the room.

Phil paused. In the corner, just in view was a foot. It was bare. He edged forward, the lantern casting its glow further. There was a leg, a body, a crouched head draped in long dark hair. Lying on the floor, hunched in the corner, cowering, arms wrapped over her face was the girl.

Placing the lamp on the floor, Phil lowered himself to his knees by the girl's side. He touched her cheek as she trembled. He could feel her freezing cold, as she wept.

'It's OK. I'm here. Come on let's get you back.'

Phil lifted the girl into his arms and carried her to the door. As he approached John entered followed by Tom. Lanterns in hand, both looking drenched. John spluttered, struggling to catch his breath.

'Look who I bumped into.'

John and Tom both looked down at the girl cradled in Phil's arms. John spoke.

'Thank God, you've found her. Was she in here all along?'

Phil replied.

'Aye. I found her hiding in the corner. Something's spooked her. She's in a state.'

Phil frowned at Tom.

'I thought I told everyone to stay indoors.'

Tom raised his eyebrows.

The Storm

'Sorry Phil. There was something urgent I had to do. I saw John on the way back and offered to help. How is she?'

'She's freezing. We need to get her back and warmed up quickly. Get my lamp, will you?'

As Tom moved to the back of the room John spoke.

'Do you think it's a good idea taking her back Phil?'

'What do you mean?'

'Maybe she's best off kept out of the way for the night. Me and Tom could stay here and watch her. There's blankets and I can get the fire going.'

John looked at Tom as he returned with Phil's lamp. There was a tension in the exchange, an edge. Phil sensed it.

'What is it? What's wrong?'

They stared at each other again, as John nodded and Tom spoke.

'Look Phil I'm telling you this cos you're a good friend, but you didn't hear it from me. I overheard Ella and Dot chatting in the hall after you left.'

Tom leant forward and began to whisper.

'I can't really say in front of her, but we best keep her out the way of Ella, and somewhere safe for the night. Folk won't think of coming here. Like John says, we'll keep an eye on her. Better still I can. There's no need for the two of us. You lads go see to your wives. You can come back later if need be.'

Phil looked at Tom then down at the girl. Tom had a point. If Ella was on the warpath then it was best to avoid her. Home was the first place she would come and Phil didn't want to expose Beth to anymore stress, nor Mary for that matter. Phil thought for a while then spoke.

'Let's get a fire sorted and the girl settled. Me and John'll go and see Mary and Beth. I'll come back and help out here later Tom.'

Tom nodded as John got the blankets and wrapped the girl in them. Phil placed her in a chair, and wrapped her up, then watched as Tommy lit a fire. The flames were soon bursting up the chimney, casting light and warmth into the room. The girl lay sleeping, as Phil reached down and stroked her hair. She seemed so helpless, just an innocent, a young girl, little more than a child. She so reminded him of Ellie, and in the strange orange glow it could have been her. If only Phil could get inside her head and find the truth. If only she would tell them. He was sure the girl meant no harm. She was vulnerable, needed them, she was a sign, a responsibility. Phil had saved her, and he would again. The sea had threatened to take her, and now on land the community that should protect her had become the girl's biggest danger. This had to end.

'Let's go John. Tommy, I'll be back later. Don't let anyone in.'

Tommy avoided Phil's stare as he replied, looking down at his feet.

'Don't worry Phil. She'll be safe.'

John and Phil left, making their way up the streets towards home. About halfway up the lane Phil stopped. Holding his lantern out front, Phil peered into the darkness of a side street, as his friend looked on, with a puzzled expression.

'What is it Phil?'

Edging towards the narrow entrance to the street, Phil's lantern spread its light into the darkness. Reaching out, clutching at the night. Phil stopped. Standing by the entrance to a lane to the right was a

The Storm

dark shadowy figure. It was difficult to see, but Phil knew who it was. The figure was Ellie. John crept by his friend's shoulder and whispered.

'What's up Phil?'

Staring into the darkness, Phil looked away and back again. He wanted to be sure it was her, that she was there. The figure remained, staring back, arms by her side, face void of emotion or expression. Phil was torn. He needed to get back and see Mary, make sure she and the baby, and Beth were safe. His job was to protect them, but there was something he needed to finish, a chapter he had to close. Now was the moment. Phil looked down at John.

'You go back. I'll follow you. Tell Mary not to worry, I won't be long. There's something I have to do.'

John stared back, confused, following Phil's line of sight to see what his friend had seen. Phil had seen something, but all John could see was the black, empty shadows of the lane. The two men waited as the storm swirled around them. John spoke first.

'Are you sure everything's alright Phil?'

'I'm fine. Trust me. This won't take long. It's something I should have done a long time ago.'

Phil looked back across the lane, but Ellie was gone. John looked on as his friend made off into the lane. He paused a moment then headed towards home. Phil was soon at the edge of the village, where the streets ended and the grassy knoll stretched out towards the church gates. The silhouette of the steeple stood watch, towering over the village beyond, as the wind howled sweeping from the sea, leaping over the wall and weaving its way between the gravestones. Phil pressed on through the gale, at every moment rising in ferocity. Entering the gate, Phil followed the path towards the right corner of the churchyard. His path was buried in darkness, with only the weak glow of his lantern to guide him. The sounds of the storm were unsettling, heightened by the reminders of death that surrounded him. Villagers spoke of ghosts and spirits that haunted the graveyard, there had been many sightings over the years. Phil never believed them. Ghosts were the souls of loved ones you kept locked inside you. That was how they lived on. The dead did not return. Then she came. His drowned daughter Ellie had returned. Now Phil knew that sometimes the dead leave before their time, with unfinished business, things that need to be resolved.

The pale yellow light dragged him further and further towards his destination. Leaving the path, Phil moved in and out of the gravestones, the stone memories of family and friends, fragments of community rotting beneath his feet. Phil slowed as he saw his daughter, the lantern bathing her in its glow. She was standing at the foot of a grave, her own grave, staring at a small bunch of flowers lying on the grass. They had withered and died, the petals a once glorious gold now brown.

Phil waited, lantern held high, the wind still dancing all around. Ellie said nothing, remaining still, eyes fixed upon the grave in front of her. Phil was overcome with a cold feeling, an icy shiver running through his body, sucking away his breath. A vision swamped his mind. It was a bright day. He was on the beach, sitting on the sand, looking out to the crystal blue sea, shimmering in the blazing sunshine. Phil shaded his eyes, and watched as the silhouette of a small girl paddled in the water, laughing, screaming, splashing. There was someone by her, a woman. Phil

The Storm

knew who they were. It was Mary and Ellie. His world. The warmth inside matched the heat of the summer sun. Mother and daughter were running towards him, the sun still stabbing at his eyes as they approached. Ellie flopped into the sand by his side, Mary soon followed. Rolling in the sand, they wrestled, Phil watching as the golden grains clung to their bodies.

The image faded, to be replaced by another. Phil and Ellie were in a boat, alone in the vast blue desert of shimmering water. She was smiling, a fishing rod in hand, waiting for something to bite. Overcome with the giddy excitement of youth, she was singing, a nursery rhyme - row, row, row your boat. Phil looked on, pipe in hand, feeling the gentle sway of the boat, drifting in and out of sleep. The warmth inside him returned, the feeling that only comes when there is love, the purest unconditional love, the love of a parent for their child. He felt an overwhelming urge to reach out to his daughter, to wrap her in his arms, protect her. Then an icy spear pierced his heart again. The blade ripped through him, writhing and twisting, as he gasped for air. The vision melted and darkness returned.

Ellie remained standing in silence. She had turned to face Phil now, watching as tears fell down her father's cheeks. She waited without a word as Phil wiped his eyes and spoke, his voice a broken whisper.

'I'm sorry Ellie, please forgive me. I'm so sorry.'

Lowering his head Phil fell to his knees and sobbed. The lantern dropped to the floor by his side, as he placed his head in his hands. As first Phil didn't notice, he was so consumed by remorse and grief. Then he felt his daughter's hand, resting on his shoulder as she stood over him. Phil lifted his head and looked into her eyes. The blank stare was now replaced by eyes sparkling with light. Phil gazed at her soft porcelain skin, her hair tied in bunches with pink ribbon. He could see her dress was now a fresh and clean bright blue. This was the fragile beauty he remembered. This was his child, his Ellie. Her red lips were stretched into the broadest of smiles. The touch of her happiness thawed the ice inside him, a rush of warmth now flowing within. Phil's tears dried up and the guilt and loathing began to dissolve. As her smile continued to beam down, Phil felt his daughter, washing the pain, healing him.

Phil was desperate to speak, trying to drag the words from his chest, past the dry wall blocking his throat. Ellie leant forward and kissed her father's forehead. A wave of love swept through his body, as she began to drift away from him. A golden aura enveloped her, then a silvery haze as his daughter began to disappear. Soon there was nothing but a faint translucent glow, only the echo of her presence remained. Phil uttered out a few final, frantic words before his daughter left him for the final time.

'Wait! Don't go!'

She was gone. Still on his knees, Phil lowered his head, closed his eyes and tried to capture her image in his mind. He wanted to hold that final image, her radiance and smile. He caught it, concentrating on the shimmering picture of her face, burning the vision in his mind. This was how Phil wanted to remember her. He had found what he had been searching for.

All consciousness slipped away, as Phil rolled over and flopped onto the grave. Curling his legs into his body, he lay like an unborn child in the womb. Water seeped through Phil's clothes, his lips touching the petals of the wilted flowers.

The Storm

....

That night the cry came, the cry of the sea. Like the mournful weeping of a lost child. The whole village heard it. Men peered through cracks in curtains into the bleak, windswept darkness while women tucked their children in extra tight. Wrapped up in bed, huddled under blankets, two young girls pretended to sleep. They heard the touch of their aunt's hand as she swept away the veil, and the creak of the floorboard as she left. They listened to their gentle breathing, each warmed by the sweet breath of the other sister. In the background, somewhere in the distance across the moor they too heard the cry. The elder sister put her arm around her younger sibling, feeling her trembling body. The younger girl whispered, little more than air wrapped around words.

'What is it?'

There was a long pause, then the elder girl answered.

'They're coming.'

The oldest sister began to sing, the softest, sweetest voice.

'Dark girl, strange girl
Where is't that you do come?
Beware the sons of fishermen
For the sea is where I'm from

Dark girl, strange girl
Why is't that you do cry?
I am longing for family
In dark water they do lie'

Dark girl, strange girl

What mischief is't you make?
Beware...

'Ssshhhhh!'
The younger sister interrupted.
'Don't say their name! You know we don't say their name!'
The elder girl laughed and continued singing.

'I am the Selkie
Your unborn babes are what I'll take'

20

John looked to the sky as it opened up with the chorus of wailing. He was on the final bend of the lane before reaching Phil's cottage. Out of breath, his chest heaving, he leant back against a wall and listened. John knew the sound, it was the same the night of the fire, the cry that came from the sea as the girl burned. He rushed to Phil's, tapped on the door, and waited. Mary's muffled voice came from the other side.

'It's me John. Open up.'

The door opened and Mary looked on, her face ashen.

'Where's Phil?'

John stepped inside and removed his jacket, as Mary locked and bolted the door.

'He said there was something he had to do, but he won't be long. He said not to worry.'

Mary took his jacket, dripping water on the floor as she laid it on the back of a kitchen chair, Mary turned to face John, the grave look still etched on her face.

'And the girl?'

'She's OK. We found her. She's at the rocket house. Tommy's watching her. We thought it best if we kept her out of the way for the night, just till things quieten down.'

John moved across to Beth who was sleeping in one of the armchairs by the fire. Falling to his knees he laid his arm against the chair and stroked her hair. He looked back at Mary and whispered.

'How is she?'

Mary nodded and smiled.

'She's fine.'

Moving round to the fire, Mary took a long iron poker and prodded the burning embers. The flames hissed and flared as the oxygen burst through the cracks. A blaze of heat surged into the room and blasted Mary's face as she spoke.

'Where did he say he was going?'

John shrugged.

'He didn't say, just that it was something he should have done a long time ago.'

Mary frowned, staring into the fire with a vacant stare. She nodded.

'I think I know where he is.'

Mary sat in an armchair, as both her and John gazed at Beth as she slept. Beth's expression was so peaceful, lost in the world of dreams, safe and protected from the tyranny of the waking world. Outside they could hear the wailing and crying as it got louder, more intense, higher in pitch. Each cry sounding more desperate than the last. They listened to the change, the rising frenzy in the cries, staring at each other with worried frowns. Mary spoke.

'It's them. They're coming.'

John lowered his head.

'I think it is Mary. It's the same sound as the other night, after the fire. But worse.'

He paused for a moment.

'Like Phil said we just sit tight and see out the night.'

Mary got to her feet and began to pace the room. The fragile flames of candles wrestled with the draughts pushing through the cracks in windows and under the door. Howling gusts whistled through the rafters and the large candle on the kitchen table blew out. Mary lit it with another, and jumped with fright as there was a banging at the door. Beth jerked upright in the armchair. She let out a shriek, still half asleep. Mary moved to the door and leant her ear towards it.

'Who is it?'

A familiar voice answered. Though the harsh tone and acid tongue were muffled, it was unmistakable.

'It's me!'

Mary looked across at John and Beth. John's expression was grim. Mary spoke.

'I have to let her in.'

John grimaced and shook his head.

'I wouldn't if I were you. If Phil gets back and finds her here there'll be war on.'

Mary hesitated, as the banging came again. Slipping the bolt back, she turned the key. Wind and rain blasted through the door as she pulled it open. Both Ella and Dot entered, looking battered by the weather. Mary glared at her nan and spoke.

'What're you doing here? Phil will be back soon and he can't find you here.'

'I won't be long.'

As Mary closed the door, she paused, and listened to the wailing from across the moor. The haunting, terrifying sound ebbed and flowed as it sailed on the waves of the wind. Through a narrow crack in the door, Mary peered out into the darkness. The streets were silent, deserted, but a shiver swept through her. It was the feeling there were eyes out there, someone was watching. Straining her eyes, reaching into the black of the night she felt sure there were movements in the shadows. There was a twinge in her abdomen, then another, this time sharper, more piercing, like a dagger being thrust into her. Struggling to catch her breath Mary slammed the door shut and bolted it.

Ella and Dot both stood with their backs to the fire, soaking up the heat, trying to revive their creaky old bones. John looked on, exchanging concerned looks with Mary. He made no attempt to disguise his disappointment, and simmering anger. Mary edged towards her nan.

'OK. What is it you want?'

Ella's voice was calm, her words precise. She knew there was only the briefest opportunity to convince Mary.

'I know I won't get through to Phil, but you Mary. I know you're worried about the girl. We have to end this. Where is she?'

Mary shook her head.

'No nan. This has all gotten out of hand. You're wrong. I was wrong. We're all confused. Phil's got everything in hand.'

'Listen woman! Can you hear that sound outside? You know what it is, and what it means.'

The wailing cries swept through the rafters, carried on the howling wind.

'It's their cry, the Selkie. They took your sister and your mother's sister. She was my youngest, barely a week old and they came in the night and took her from me. You of all people know how that feels Mary, to lose a child. No mother should ever have to suffer that. I won't let it happen again. I'm putting an end to this. Now, where is the girl?'

The cries continued to howl through the cracks as Ella's words hit Mary. She knew how it felt to lose a child, of the pain that never goes away. She had to live with it everyday. Mary never knew she had a sister, or an aunt that might have been. Looking at her nan, Mary saw the heartache and anger in her eyes. Beyond the harsh scowl and weathered skin there lay a lifetime of suffering. The women carried the pain of loss, and few communities had more suffering thrust upon them than those that fished the sea. Ella's pain had not made her hate, or seek to harm, it had taught her to protect, especially her own. It had shown her the importance of family, friends, and community. Always, and at any cost.

There was another stabbing pain in Mary's stomach. Then another, as she winced, and grabbed her side. Losing her breath, Mary felt her legs buckle, as Ella rushed towards her.

'What is it Mary?'

'I'm fine. It's just a little pain. I should sit down'

Mary grabbed Ella's arm, as her nan helped her stand. Together they shuffled towards the bed. John and Beth huddled round her, and Beth spoke.

'Where's the pain Mary?'

Mary let out a cry and fell onto the bed, writhing in agony, clutching her stomach. Ella grabbed her granddaughter's arm.

'What's wrong Mary? Where's the pain?'

Mary whimpered and moaned, then screamed pulling her legs tight into her body as she wept. She cried out, desperate, drowning the cries from outside.

'It's the baby! Please God no. Not again. Please don't take another one.'

Mary squeezed the words out, through the wall of pain. Ella looked around at the others, a look of confusion, questioning. Dot looked shocked, her creased weather-worn face was ashen. Beth was frantic, racked with worry and close to tears. The confusion on Ella's face soon disappeared, replaced with anger and heartache. She was bleeding for her granddaughter, desperate to ease the suffering. The old woman had seen this many times, had to endure the same herself.

An image flashed into Ella's mind, a face. Anger swept through her body, as she heard the muttering of voices in her head - friends, family, neighbours, loose tongues voicing dark thoughts.

'She brought this on herself. It's all her fault.'

'Did you see the look on her face? She's cursed.'

'She's cast a spell on Mary. She's one of them.'

'That's what the girl's come for. The baby. That's what they want - to take our men and children.'

'We have to send her back to where she belongs.'

'She doesn't belong here.'

The words echoed over and over, babble, chatter, baying for blood, her blood, the girl sent to them, the dark haired girl, the mysterious girl, the Selkie.

Anger simmered in Ella's eyes, as she bit her lip and cursed under her gin stained breath. The fire of her anger had turned into a burning desire to act. The emotion raged deep inside her as she watched Mary twist and scream. A tear ran down Ella's face, creeping from the corner of her eye. Trickling down her rugged cheek, rolling over the folds in her skin, it mingled with the cold sweat dripping from her brow. Ella stepped away from the bed and let out a cry that cut through the room. Beth jumped in shock, while Dot looked on in horror. John put his arm on the old woman's shoulder.

'Are you OK Ella?'

Mary thrust her head back, teeth clenched, eyes bulging, bleeding tears. Ella looked down at the sheets below and noticed a pool of fresh, crimson blood. The old woman handed a cloth to Beth, and thrust a glance at John.

'Where is she?'

The Storm

John shook his head, as Ella scowled and pressed her face close to his, spitting out the words again.

'I'll ask you once more John. Where is she?'

Sweat trickled down John's brow, and he shuddered as he looked at Beth. His wife nodded and then looked away. John stared back at the old woman, noticing her fist clenched by her side, as her eyes bore holes in him. Mary screamed again, a harrowing wail of anguish, as Beth shouted.

'For God's sake tell her man.'

In the panic John blurted out the words.

'The rocket house.'

Ella turned to Dot.

'See to Mary. There's something I need to take care of.'

Ella pushed past John and stormed out of the door. The old woman darted through the streets, oblivious to the storm. Dark clouds pressed down, as the gales battered the windows and rushed through the open doorway, sucking the rain inside. The narrow lanes remained deserted, the only sounds the storm, and the clatter of Ella's wooden soles against the cobbles.

Reaching through the door to the rocket house, Ella slipped inside. Tommy sat in the corner by the fire, smoking a pipe, drifting in and out of sleep. The girl was huddled in the chair, wide awake, eyes fixed on the floor, arms clasped around her body. Ella made straight towards the girl, grabbing her by the dark strands of hair. The girl screamed as the old woman dragged her to her feet. Tommy jumped from his chair and reached for Ella, gripping her arm.

'Go easy on her Ella.'

With a look of disdain, Ella brushed his hand aside, squaring up to the young man, as she held the terrified girl.

'Don't try and stop me Tommy. I'm doing what someone should have done from the start. She doesn't belong here. She's brought her curses, witchcraft, and evil to the village. She's going back where she belongs.'

'Wait Ella. What are you going to do with her? Don't do anything stupid. Think about it woman. She's just a bloody kid.'

Ella scowled at Tommy as she yanked the girl's hair. The girl let out a cry, looking at Tommy, eyes pleading for help. Ella's stare was fixed on the young man.

'She's no girl Tommy. She's one of them. They've sent her, to divide us, so we fight amongst ourselves. That's how they work. They turn us against our own so they can take what they need when we're weak. Look what they've taken already. I won't let them take any more. I won't let them take my Mary's child.'

Tommy edged his body between Ella and the door, as she tried to steer round him.

'Wait. We'll speak to Phil. He'll know what to do. He'll make sure Mary and the bairn aren't in any danger. Come on Ella.'

Ella spat her words at Tommy as he shuffled to try and block her path.

'There's no point. Phil's a good man, but he's weak. He won't see the truth. Now get out of my way.'

Tommy's face was filled with defiance, as Ella stared back at him. The old woman tugged at the girl's hair again. The girl let out a scream. Staring at Tommy, tears flooding down her cheeks, the girl's face

The Storm

was locked in a desperate plea. Meanwhile Ella raised her clenched fist and held it towards Tommy's chin.

'Are you really going to try and stop me Thomas Arkle? Just remember who you're talking to lad. I used to give you a good beating when you were a child and I'll do it again if I have to. Now are you going to move?'

The eyes of old and young remained locked together, a silent duel, neither willing to back down. Ella waited, then barked at Tommy one last threat.

'This is your last chance Tommy. Move!'

The old woman spat the words out, while the girl hung like a rag doll at Ella's shoulder, head arched as Ella clutched and tugged at her hair. Tommy looked down at Ella, puffing his chest out further, and twisting his face in a sneer. Ella struck him, hard in the face. This was no gentle slap, but a punch, bang against his jaw. Tommy's head spun to one side, as his legs buckled and he folded over and fell to his knees. The young man lay on the floor holding his face. Ella stared down at him, waiting to see if he would respond, her fist ready to strike again. Tommy stayed crouched on the floor, not daring to look the old woman in the eye, nursing his wounded jaw and pride. Ella spoke, her voice calm, but menacing.

'You'll get another one if you try and stop me. Now stay here.'

Ella yanked at the girl as she would the rope of a dog, dragging her towards the door. All the while the old woman muttered and cursed to herself, in between barking at the girl. They reached the door, Ella pausing to look down at her.

'You're going back where you belong.'

21

Phil woke, still lying on the soaked grass, as needles of rainwater stung his face. He heard the sound, the cry sweeping over the blackened sky, rolling and tumbling with the wind. Phil realised where he was, and began to remember how he got there. Sitting up and looking around, the lantern still glowed beside him, its flame weak and spluttering, dying. A tiny gravestone stood at his feet. On it was carved an inscription, a simple tribute, all they could afford, a name and two dates. Images of the hours before came back to him, Ellie's face, the smile. Phil knew it was over, he could move on. Now it was only about Mary, him, and the baby. The wailing in the sky grew louder, the storm more intense. The cries came from the sea, way beyond the church. This was a warning. They were coming. Phil knew it now. He had to protect Mary and the baby.

....

Bursting through the door, Phil hurled his overcoat on the floor and dashed to the bed. He could hear Mary's cries, see her writhing in agony, the screams drowning the wailing from outside. His wife's face was twisted, her teeth clenched, as she lay dripping in pools of crimson sweat. There was blood everywhere, the bed, her nightgown, the sheets were stained in the darkest red. Phil fell to his knees and took Mary's hand. She opened her eyes, realising her husband had returned and was now by her side. Mary spoke, her voice weary.

'Phil! Phil! The baby!'

'It's OK. I'm here. You're going to be fine.'

The Storm

Phil looked at Beth who was pressing a cool, damp cloth against Mary's forehead. John stood looking on, feeling every bit of Mary's pain, wincing with every cry. Behind him Dot watched, silent and stone faced. Phil caught the old woman's eye.

'What are you doing here? You're not welcome. Now go!'

John turned and gestured towards the door. Dot sighed and nodded, as Beth spoke.

'Wait Phil. I could really do with some help here. Dot knows what she's doing. She'll have seen this many times before.'

Phil stared at Beth, then glared back at Dot, as Mary let out a scream that ripped through them all. Gripping his wife's hand as tight as he could, Phil urged her to squeeze it, wanting to absorb her pain, somehow take it from her. Still gazing down at Mary, Phil spoke, unable to hide his anger and discomfort.

'OK. She can stay for now.'

Dot sprung into action, taking a bowl from the bedside and filling it with fresh water. She began rifling through the cupboards, pulling out random jars. The old woman knew what she wanted, working without hesitation. She placed various powders and leaves into a cup and stirred, then returned to the bed barging past Beth to reach the screaming patient. Dot looked at Phil.

'I've made something that'll help her. We'll leave it for a few minutes, then get her to drink it. It should help ease the pain.'

They all stared at Mary and waited, as her screams eased, and the pain subsided. Dot gestured to Beth.

'Bring the cup Beth. It's time.'

Beth moved to the table, as Dot helped Mary sit up. Beth passed the old woman the cup. Dot placed it against Mary's lips and fed her the liquid. Phil watched as his wife gulped, her face curdling at the taste. Dot spoke.

'Drink it all Mary. It'll do you good.'

Once assured the cup was empty, Dot lowered Mary back into a lying position, and began to stroke her forehead. The old woman's caress was loving, tender, a side others seldom saw. Mary drifted off to sleep, the crying stopped, and the pain melted from her face. Phil still knelt by his wife's side, holding her hand as he leant across and whispered to the old woman.

'Thank you.'

Dot smiled as she got to her feet and moved back to the kitchen. The old woman began busying herself clearing away. Beth joined her as John knelt down and whispered in Phil's ear.

'I know this isn't the best time, but Ella was here before. She left just before you arrived.'

Phil glared at John.

'Where is she now?'

John lowered his head.

'I don't know. She saw what was happening with Mary and the baby and left.'

Phil jumped to his feet.

'Did she mention the girl?'

John looked back at Phil and frowned. Phil grabbed his coat and made for the door, John close behind. As the two men were about to leave Dot shouted.

'Let's hope you're not too late.'

Phil stared back at the old woman.

'What do you mean?'

Dot grinned and nodded.

'Ella knows what needs to be done.'

Phil and John sped through the door and into the storm. Beth closed the door behind them, turned and pressed her back against it. Staring back at Dot she saw the grin still etched on the old woman's face.

....

The girl screamed and wailed, cries of fear and desperation, as Ella dragged her down the jetty and onto the beach. A few women had heard the cries and were running towards them. They sprang from the houses at the lower end of the street, just behind the boatyard. Word was out, and news of the commotion were spreading like fire through the tight knit community. Others had heard the screams and were coming to investigate. A small crowd was building, following, but careful not to intervene. Whatever they thought of Ella and her actions, none were brave enough to stop her.

The storm continued to rage around them, growing in ferocity all the time. The frozen rain spat its sharp needles, each biting and stinging into the skins of the crowd. The sea continued to wail and cry, louder and more desperate than ever. The girl struggled with Ella, desperate to break free. The old woman was too strong, fuelled by her determination and anger. Pressing her legs deep into the sand, the girl pulled against Ella who continued their march towards the raging sea. Ella paused and grabbed the girl's hair with both hands, staring at her victim, menace in the old woman's face. The girl's eyes blazed with fear as Ella gripped even harder, jerking her head back. The girl's legs buckled with the jolt, and Ella began to move again. The old woman's stride was strong, the anger still boiling within, driving her onwards.

The crowd was building behind them. Almost all were women, with only a smattering of men and children. They had heard the cries, first of the sea, then of the girl. Some had peeked from behind drawn curtains and seen the shadows of Ella dragging the screaming girl onto the beach. Others had responded to knocks on the door, and excited neighbours urging them to come. The crowd followed Ella, keeping a cautious distance. They were all anxious to see the drama unfold, each knowing how this would end.

Meanwhile, Tommy had brushed off his wounded chin and gone to find Phil. The young man had made a big mistake, and knew it. He had let his friend down and it was time to make amends. Tommy never thought Ella would go this far. Only Phil could stop this now. Only he could talk any sense into her. Only he had the strength and courage to prevent her from this madness.

Ella and the girl edged closer to the sea, while in the crowd a nervous excitement grew. Tension was mixed with the desperate cries of the girl and the sea, wrapped in the cacophony of wind, rain, and waves. The old woman reached the water, the waves roaring and crashing into the sand. Ella waded into the raging sea without hesitation or fear, as though it wasn't there. The cries of the girl became more frantic, the icy waters now tumbling at her feet. She twisted and turned, her hands grabbing at Ella, scratching at the leather skin, crushing the gnarled fingers, still unable to loosen the old woman's iron grip. Ella surged on through the waves. Step by step, inching forward into the watery grave. Soon they were up to their waists, the girl lost her footing and plunged into the foaming sea. Ella held on, refusing to let her prisoner get away, still clutching her hair, and dragging her head above

The Storm

the water while the girl gasped for breath. Spitting the salty water from her mouth, the girl tried to clear her lungs. As she struggled to free herself, the girl's cries began to change, replaced by fragments of words, a strange language. The sounds were gibberish to Ella, they meant nothing, all pleading lost on the stubborn old woman.

The crowd of onlookers at the waters edge was growing. Ripples of tension ran through them, excited chatter, the occasional holler and yell.

'Get rid of her Ella. She's cursed.'

'Send her back to where she belongs!'

Beyond the lifeboat station, at the start of the narrow, winding streets someone was shouting. It was an unmistakable voice, a booming sound bellowing deep from the lungs of a giant frame. Phil hurtled down the end of the lane, towards the beach, followed by Tommy and John. His voice surged through the air, piercing the wall of sound from the storm, reaching the crowd, and then Ella.

'Stop! No! For Christ's sake Ella. No!'

Phil bounded across the beach towards the water, pounding the heavy, rain sodden sand. All the while Phil shouted, pleading with the old woman, his voice growing in desperation as he neared the crowd.

'Stop her. Come on. Don't just stand there. Somebody do something!'

The crowd watched Phil approach, shifting their gaze between him and the unfolding drama in the waves. The waters were smashing at Ella's chest now, only her head and shoulders could be seen between the tumble and swirl of the sea. The girl's head burst from the water, coughing, spluttering, gasping for air. Her skin was a pinky blue, seared from the blades of arctic water slicing at her face and body. She continued to plead in her strange foreign tongue, as Ella pushed on.

The old woman paused, only for the briefest of moments, a flash of mercy swept through her. In that faintest glimmer all anger subsided, and Ella was overcome by pity and forgiveness. She looked back at the girl who saw the softening in the old woman's eyes. Sadness mixed with sorrow and doubt. Ella's grip eased, and the madness let go.

From the shore came Phil's desperate cries. Hitting the water, he surged through the waves towards them. The girl gazed deep into Ella's eyes, both their faces drenched in icy salt water. The girl's lips pressed together to form a word, her final word perhaps, a foreign word to her, but one familiar to Ella.

'Please!'

At that moment Ella knew, and all the anger swept from her body and into the water. The old woman and the girl's eyes locked together, and a huge wave bore down upon them, just as Phil was within their reach. The huge wall of water towered above, Ella dragged the girl behind her, stretching out her arms like a cross, of forgiveness and protection. Time seemed to slow, the waves tumbling and rolling over them. Ella could still hear Phil's desperate cry as he lunged forward and grabbed the girl. It was then Ella let out her final words, the full force of the water striking her. Phil heard Ella's last desperate plea.

'Forgive me.'

The wall of freezing water dragged Ella under. Phil and the girl also felt its force, almost knocking them over and pulling them under into its dark depths. Phil stood firm, using all his strength to fight the water as it crashed around them. The torrent subsided, and Phil stood clutching the girl in his arms.

He passed the girl to John who carried her to the safety of the shore. Phil reached out and grasped in the water, searching, grabbing all around him, desperate to find Ella. He cried out the old woman's name, racked with anguish.

'Ella. Ella.'

Another wave returned, sweeping over him, thrusting him from side to side. All the while he fought on, scrambling in the water, calling out her name, refusing to give in. Beneath the dark waters, Ella lay, overcome with a dreamlike serenity. All was calm in the icy depths, despite the madness of the storm and tumbling waves above. The old woman plunged to the sea floor, and gazed back up at the surface. She could see the silhouette of Phil's body, his hands reaching below, searching for her. Ella reached out for his hand, stretching as far as she could, their fingertips almost touching. Then Ella felt something grab her, strong arms tightening around her waist, sweeping her away, just as Phil and Ella were about to touch.

She watched Phil's hands fade away, her arms still outstretched. His silhouette disappeared, and Ella saw strange translucent shapes swirling around her. Long strands of black hair twirled in the waters, caressing pale white skin. The faces of young, girls with soft angelic features swept past the old woman. Ella felt a hand grip her ankle. She looked down and saw the white fingers locked around her leg. Small air bubbles burst from the old woman's mouth. Her last breath. Ella was swept away, a single hand leading her to the darkest corners of the sea. Away from the shore, and the arms of Phil. Away from her home, and all she had known and loved. Away from her Mary.

Phil scrambled in the water. Wave after wave struck his body, but none were strong enough to fell him. His frantic search was beginning to wane, his arms tiring, facing the growing realisation it was all over. Just then a different crying and wailing came from the sea. It was slow and steady, but grew in volume and intensity. Soon a blanket of sound enveloped the whole of the bay, soaring over the roar of the waves and thunder, of the wind and rain. A long line of villagers crowded the shoreline, each mesmerised by this strange, enchanting sound. It was eery, unsettling, but compelling. All eyes gazed out, transfixed on the music of the sea as it wept.

It was then he appeared. A shadow in the distance, emerging from the water above the rolling waves, a silhouette creeping towards the shore. The villagers saw the figure moving towards them. They looked on, still hypnotised by the music of the wailing sea, the waves dancing amidst the symphony of the storm. Striding forth through the dark, tumbling water, the silhouette drew closer. Then the people saw his blank stare and vacant expression. He had returned, released, saved from the creatures, freed from his prison of the sea.

Young Tom edged forward through the waves, hands by his side, surging through the icy water towards the beach. The villagers watched, a mixture of horror and excitement. The shadowy figure crept closer into view, nearing the shore and stepping from the water onto the beach. The people awoke from their stupor, surging forward towards the returned, grabbing each other, hugging and cheering. Tom's mother had seen her son, and was running to greet him along with the others. The villagers gathered round Tom, collapsed to his knees on the windswept sands, his mother crouched alongside, arms wrapped around him, sobbing.

Tom looked dazed and lifeless. He said nothing, just stared at the cold sand. After a while he looked up, and stared at all those looking down at him. His eyes began to spark back to life, as though a flame had been lit. Shaking his head, the young boy's gaze swept around the villagers in confusion. Dazed and overwhelmed, but all the while beginning to realise he was alive, and home. Phil looked on, mouth open in disbelief, still overcome by the despair of losing Ella, but feeling fragments of joy and relief at Tom's return.

Phil noticed his body was shaking, and he began to wade back through the waves towards the beach. Pausing a moment when he reached the edge of the sand, Phil was overcome with a strange sensation. He was being watched. He turned and looked back out at the sea, where just beyond the shoreline, a line of shadowy figures nestled in the water. Phil could make out the curves of their bodies, and the long, dark hair draped beyond their shoulders. The shadows swayed upon the churning waves, all the while watching Phil and the others. The villagers remained huddled together, continuing to celebrate the return of Tom, oblivious to the figures in the water. Phil scanned the line of silhouettes, their eyes and his locked on one another, his body still trembling. The storm raged on around them, and for a moment time seemed to slow, creeping to a standstill. Phil felt all consciousness slipping away, as exhaustion began to surge through him. Fighting to stay awake, the last fragments of strength were gone, and he collapsed in a heap on the sand. One by one, the dark figures turned and slipped into the sea.

Chris Ord

DAY SIX

Chris Ord

22

The storm had ended, replaced by flashes of a crisp, bright sun of late winter. Black clouds still hung over the village but these were different clouds. These were clouds that were dissolving, soon to be gone. At the first sign of calm, Phil had left and taken a horse and cart to the market town of Morpeth. It was only a distance of twelve miles, but the road was still hazardous, the ravages of the storm leaving wounds that would take time to heal.

Late that evening Phil returned to the village. Calling to check on Mary, then heading for the church where a service was being held for the victims of the storm. Phil entered the wooden doors and made his way along the central aisle. The pews were packed, as the whole community had come to pay their respects. This was not just the fisher folk, but tradesmen, professionals, people from all walks of life, each united in grief. All the families of the victims were there, all except Mary and the girl. The people of the village were joined by Tom, who remembered nothing of his ordeal beneath the waves, the prisoner of the Selkie. He was thankful to be alive, but in time dark memories would return, most often while he slept.

The vicar stood at the pulpit addressing the congregation. As Phil walked the aisle, the heads of each row turned. The vicar stopped the sermon as he approached. Looking down from the pulpit, Father Matthew waited while Phil removed his hat, twisting it in his hands. Casting his eyes across the congregation, Phil nodded, a nervous acknowledgement, a sea of familiar faces. The vicar stepped down and took Phil's hand.

'How are Mary and the girl?'

'Both doing as well as you'd expect.'

'And the baby?'

The vicar placed his arm on Phil's shoulder who lowered his head, fighting back the tears. After a moment, Phil spoke, his voice a cracked whisper.

'May I speak Matthew?'

'Of course.'

Father Matthew stepped back and Phil turned to address the people in the church. All eyes were transfixed, mouths open in anticipation. Phil cleared his throat.

'Good evening everyone.'

Phil steadied himself, took a deep breath, and continued.

'I went to Morpeth today, to report the wreck of the Embla, and tell them that the crew were lost. I didn't tell them the whole story, just what they needed to know. I think there are things that need to stay here, with us.'

Phil looked up, his eyes sweeping across the heads of the congregation, capturing the glances, the nods and the occasional knowing stare.

'They gave me a list of the crew and passengers. I have it here.'

Phil took a piece of paper from his pocket, unfolded it and held it above his head.

'All the crewmen are named and the captain, Jens Christian.'

Phil paused for a moment, composing himself again, the words proving more difficult. He looked out into the congregation catching sight of young Tom.

'I can't explain what has happened these past few days. I'm not sure we'll ever know, but it'll stay with us all for a long time. You'll tell your children about this and the stories will be passed down through them. People will think it's just a story, a folk tale, nothing more. But we'll know different. We know what we've lived through, what we saw, what we lost.'

Pausing again, Phil cleared his throat.

'There's one more thing.'

As he looked out at the faces staring at him he saw a sea of people he knew and loved. People he had grown up with, worked with, lives he had saved.

'There was another name on the list, a young girl.'

The words struck them like arrows, one by one. Frowns and confusion swept across the faces of the congregation. Phil caught a few eyes, while others lowered their heads, many looked away.

'Her name is Sophia.'

Phil looked around the faces again. Most avoided him, coughs echoed around the cavern of the old stone church. An uncomfortable silence hung in the chilly air of the chancel. Everyone waited, including Father Matthew who stood behind, head aloft gazing at the ancient wooden beams. After a long while Phil continued.

'The girl joined the crew at Whitby and was taking passage back home to Holland.'

Phil lowered his head as his voice began to crack.

'Sophia is with child.'

Phil's voice grew louder, more commanding, struggling to contain his anger.

'There's a lot happened to us all these past few days. A lot for us all to think about.'

Phil waited a moment, let his words resonate around the cold room, looking across the sea of familiar faces.

'Let's learn from this.'

Phil allowed the words to find their mark, giving everyone time to absorb their meaning.

'We've lost Ella. In the end she came to realise she was wrong. She gave her life to save the girl.'

As Phil lowered his head, the congregation remained silent, some staring at the floor, others into the emptiness in the corners of the room. All were lost in thought, locked in prayer, each holding the image of a sullen old woman in their mind. Phil took a deep breath.

'Some of you risked your lives to save the crew of the Embla. We failed, but...'

Phil cleared his throat again, gathering himself before he spoke again.

'Be proud we tried.'

No more words were needed. Everyone knew what was left unsaid. Phil looked out across the people, instead of eyes and faces all he could see were the tops of heads. His words hung in the air like the thick, black clouds of the storm. Phil turned and reached out to shake the hand of the vicar. Both men made their way along the aisle towards the door. As they shuffled forward, side by side, step by step, the heads in the church remained bowed, facing forward.

Phil and the vicar left the ancient walls and moved along the dark, narrow path of the churchyard. They walked in silence for a while, but nearing the gate Matthew spoke.

'Give Mary my love.'

Phil looked down at the stone cobbles.

'She'll be fine.'

Phil's voice broke. He took a deep breath.

'We lost the baby.'

Matthew rested his hand on Phil's shoulder, looking on as Phil let the tears flow. The vicar waited, letting all the emotion flood from his friend. After a while Matthew spoke.

'I'm sorry Phil. So, so sorry.'

There was silence, before Matthew continued.

'Mary is strong. She'll recover and there will be other children.'

Phil averted the vicar's comforting stare. Instead, he fumbled with his hat. Matthew spoke again.

'I'm sorry about Ella too. She was a brave woman, and a good woman. She showed us all in the end. You can be proud of her.'

Phil looked up and frowned.

'I should never have let it get that far.'

The two men stood for a moment, gazing into the hazy darkness, chasing the shadows that danced beneath the silhouettes of the church. In the background they could hear the rolling waves of the sea crashing into the rocks beyond. Matthew spoke, his voice soft, the music of his words soothing.

'Things have happened none of us can explain, but let's not be too harsh on anyone. You can understand why we were all afraid. They're good people. You know that.'

The two men exchanged knowing looks and Phil spoke.

'We're only ever as good as the things we do.'

Phil's voice tailed off into a cracked whisper. Matthew waited a moment.

'What's going to happen with the girl?'

'She'll stay with us, at least until she's had the baby. Once she's recovered we'll talk to her, try to contact her family. Maybe we can offer her a new home. It's our chance to make amends.'

Matthew nodded.

'I can think of no better place for her than with Mary and you.'

The two men shook hands, and said their farewells. Phil left the churchyard and headed for home. Hugging the stone wall, his broad, towering shadow crossed the road into the streets beyond. Head bowed, shoulders slumped, he disappeared into the cold evening.

....

A couple of days later, on a dark, dreary morning, a body washed up on the beach in the bay. It was an old woman, with grey hair strewn across gnarled, leathery skin. She was found curled in a ball, wrapped like a foetus, lying still and lifeless. Her chest no longer moved with the gentle rhythm of her breathing. Her heart no longer beat within. Her face and eyes were gone, devoured by the creatures of the sea, destroyed beyond all recognition.

Ella was buried in the churchyard, on the point of the bay looking out over the village and sea beyond. By the old stone walls her remains lay, where her beloved community worshipped, the one she had devoted her life to. Wrapped in the arms of this small piece of land, the gateway to their kingdom of eternal peace. A quiet corner of the world where generations of the familiar and forgotten rested together alone, ghosts locked in the memories of all those they had loved.

For years to come a dark haired girl would visit Ella's grave, each time laying fresh flowers. Crouching by the simple headstone, she would mumble a prayer in an odd language. Week after week this beautiful stranger and her young daughter returned. Now and then, when the wind was at its wildest and dark clouds hung heavy overhead, the girl and her daughter would not be alone. Lurking in the shadows, they would be there. Watching and waiting. Always in silence. Biding their time. Until the storm returned.

ACKNOWLEDGMENTS

I would like to thank my family, friends and all those who have supported and believed in me. You know who you are. Special thanks go to Sheila Harrison and the team at Newbiggin Maritime Centre for their on-going support.

My fascination with 'Big' Philip Jefferson began with the project 'Haalin' the Lines.' Funded by BAIT in South-East Northumberland, the project was led by the remarkable performer and singer-songwriter, Tim Dalling. Tim was commissioned by BAIT to take historical accounts being gathered by the Newbiggin-by-the-Sea Genealogy Project and put some of the stories to music. The aim was to bring back to life the tales and oral histories of local heroes in the village. One of those heroes was 'Big' Philip Jefferson, the first Newbiggin Lifeboat Coxswain who was awarded a clasp to his silver medal for an attempted service to the brig 'Embla' in 1854.

As well as Tim and the Genealogy Project team, led by Hilton Dawson, the project also involved local choir, 20,000 Voices, Newbiggin soprano singer, Susan Robertson, musical arrangers Ken Patterson and Richard Scott, and members of Jayess Newbiggin Brass Band, for which I play solo horn. We delivered a number of acclaimed performances all expertly conducted by 20,000 Voices Musical Director, Graham Coatman.

At the end of the project I was curious to find out more, and further research revealed what an incredible man Phil was. My aim in writing this story is to help Phil's legacy carry on. His is a tale of selfless heroism, an inspiration to the people of Newbiggin, a man who led a community to risk their lives for strangers. History is filled with tales of kings and queens, leaders and generals, yet the true heroes are all around us. People who build communities, live and die for their families, friends, and neighbours. What remains of them is love and memories. It is vital we keep the memories alive.

Phil and his crew of young men attempted to save the 'Embla' that stormy night in 1854. This much we know. Their valiant rescue failed. The crew of the 'Embla' all perished, and were buried in the graveyard of St Mary the Virgin Church at Woodhorn. The rest is just a story, a folk tale, words conjured from the dark chambers of my mind, and sprinkled with imagination. I hope you enjoy it and the spirit of Philip Jefferson lives on in us all.

ABOUT THE AUTHOR

Chris is a married father of four boys. After graduating in the early 90s he became an English language teacher living in Turkey, Portugal, India and traveling beyond. He returned to the UK to study an MA in International Politics and worked at Warwick University. He then moved into policy research and implementation. Currently, Chris is a Partnership Manager for the National Citizen Service, delivering outdoor activity and social action programmes for young people across the North East.

Chris is also a musician and plays solo horn for Jayess Newbiggin Brass Band, his beloved village where he grew up, and the setting for 'The Storm.' Chris loves running and in addition to a couple of marathons has run many half marathons and 10Ks. He currently lives in Monkseaton, near Newcastle upon Tyne.

Chris' dream was always to write, and his journey began in August 2015 when he took voluntary redundancy from his role in education policy. His first novel 'Becoming' was published in September 2016 to widespread acclaim. 'Becoming' is a dystopian story about a teenage girl called Gaia, and her attempt to escape a brutal community on Holy Island in Northumberland.

'The Storm' is Chris' second published novel. He also writes regular articles and observations on his blog, and his work has appeared in local newspapers and magazines. As well as delivering readings at local author events, Chris also visits schools across the country to give talks on writing. In 2017 Chris was commissioned by Woodhorn Museum to write a series of passages in support of their 'Wonderfolk' interactive family experience. His latest project is writing the follow-up to 'Becoming' entitled 'Awakening' which he hopes to release in 2018.

Further information on Chris and his work can be found at:
> http://chrisord.wixsite.com/chrisord
> or on Facebook at:
> https://www.facebook.com/chrisordauthor/

Printed in Great Britain
by Amazon